The Sunset's Shadow

Mayra M. Bermúdez-Arroyo

Hoja Fina

The Sunset's Shadow
ISBN: 978-1-7357816-4-8
© **Mayra M. Bermúdez-Arroyo**
bermudezclub@me.com
First edition English version: August 2021
Cover Graphic Art/Artistic concept: Mónica Bermúdez
Editor: Antonio de Jesús Martell
Content Corrector: Ana Loreanne Colón
Translator: Melba Ferrer

For my family ♥ past and present

If you want to fly on the sky,
you need to leave the earth.
If you want to move forward,
you need to let go the past
that drags you down."
Amit Ray

Note: In late August of 2012, the media reported that two teenagers from San Juan had gone missing. The two, unbeknownst to their parents and teachers, wanted to capture the beauty of a sunset in the eastern part of Puerto Rico. All they wanted was to take the ferry to Culebra, or perhaps to Vieques. And they would have carried out their plans, but they were unable to. They were rescued, unharmed, by authorities. This fragment of an incident spurred in the author's imagination the desire to accompany the teenagers and go through with their adventure. Any similarity to true events is pure fantasy from an author who enjoys playing the game of obscuring realities and creating sunsets.

Chapter 1 - Marisol and Guillermo

The two new adolescent faces at Terminal East in Río Piedras belonged to Marisol and Guillermo. It was their first time there.

They were in the seventh grade together at the junior high school in the Río Piedras town center. They met in the school's choir and were immediately smitten. Marisol's long hair swaying in the breeze captivated Guillermo, the way a hummingbird is captivated by the cayenne hues of the tropics. She, in turn, was enthralled by the glimmer in his olive-green eyes. It was on that day during choir practice when Marisol decided to bid farewell to the child and embrace the first whispers of womanhood. She chose, right then and there, to be a woman, with no second thoughts. The two teens had not even accidentally brushed against each other in that special way that could melt an iceberg to the very core. Cupid's arrow may have come from afar, but it hit the mark alright, immediately triggering desire. On that very first day they met, she knew she wanted to grow old with him and, he, from the tenors' section in the choir, succumbed to two words forming a woman's name: *mar* and *sol*, Marisol.

Guillermo did everything possible to sit behind her in History class. They shared their snacks during recess, and at lunch they chatted about family and school. They usually liked the same books, thriller movies, American hip-hop videos, and they loved cheese pizza. They were also amused at how they didn't like the same things: sports and Formula I races.

On the day school was over for the summer, they exchanged very saddened goodbyes, hoping the months would go by quickly so that they could see each other again.

As usual, Marisol's aunt picked her up after school at exactly three o'clock, while Guillermo walked back home with his buddies.

♥

On the first day of the new school semester, all the students chatted about their vacation. Marisol spent her summer at home watching movies because her parents were working and were unable to take time off. But Guillermo said he spent his first days ever in Vieques with his parents, assuring everyone that the sunset of many hues there is, in itself, a spectacle well worth seeing. It starts out as a huge orange globe amid such a pleasing hush and, he said, for the first time he saw vivid violets and crimsons as the sun went down.

"My father rented a jeep and we visited hidden places. On the first day, after dinner, we went for a ride. The salty breeze in my face made me drowsy. We passed by a school and I wondered what life was like for the kids in Vieques. Do they go to the beach every day? I imagined that each family had at least two horses, because they roamed freely everywhere and were quite docile. Instead of dogs or cats, the people there had horses as pets. We then passed the airport, which is small, but modern. And up ahead we saw an old *ceiba* tree. It was huge. Majestic. Its trunk looked like a towering wall. I was excited and wanted to climb up the tree and slide down its trunk, but then I remembered that I'm already thirteen and it's not good to behave like a child in front of others. We then went to Mosquito Bay. What a name, right? At the end of the road there was a fence and a guard. He was surrounded by people."

Guillermo added that, since the guard spent so much time alone, he started—just for the heck of it—amassing and piling up stones from around the area, erecting figures he called stone bonsais. Each one, he said, represented a member of a family.

"Stones?" interrupted Marisol.

"Yeah. You know, I felt sorry for him. He was really tanned by the sun and his eyes were sad. I told my father that I could never hold a job like that because I'd die of boredom. But *Papi* said that perhaps Abelardo—that was his name—was the happiest man in the entire Caribbean. I was surprised. His reply made me wonder a bit, as if I had just discovered a new truth. I felt better, though, when I saw *Mami* smile. It's those half-serious half-joking remarks that grownups make that make you wonder. We continued along the coast, passing Mosquito Bay, and to the left was the Kianí lagoon, which was closed because it was polluted. "Jerks," said *Mami*. We continued ahead to the end of the road. We were precisely at the easternmost tip of Vieques, on Punta Arenas Beach. Since we didn't have our bathing suits with us, we only walked along the shore. The water was so warm, and the breeze tousled our hair in a continuous caress. *Mami* stretched out a huge towel on the sand and the three of us watched the sunset. Such peaceful silence! You could see several sailboats, playful amid the eastern winds, and on the horizon, you could see Fajardo, the easternmost tip of Puerto Rico. *Papi* hugged us and *Mami* hushed away the silence: "We have to come back each year to appreciate all this beauty." She then laughed and cried. And then I laughed and was moved. We were there for about fifteen minutes when suddenly my mother complained of being bitten by something. The fishermen told us that it was something like a swarm, which is how they call the sand flies that come out in the evenings from the nearby mangroves. Throughout the rest of the week, we visited different beaches to capture that moment as a family. It was wonderful!"

"I want to go!" begged Marisol, her fingers entwining Guillermo's.

"Really? I guess our parents could meet and we can…"

"No! I know my mother," she paused, "won't agree. We have no money for a vacation. But we can go by ourselves," she added, squeezing his hand and looking so deeply into those olive-green eyes.

"But Baby, how?"

"We're old enough now. We can go by public transportation to the Fajardo dock. I'll check. That is, if you're up to it. Are you? Nah, you wouldn't dare. You don't look like the daring type to me."

Guillermo stared at the floor for a few seconds. He mumbled an *okay* and swallowed so hard he felt his gum going down his throat.

"Today's the fifteenth, I think," said Marisol, pulling out a school agenda from the front pocket of her backpack to pore over the month of August. "How about going at the end of the month? We can leave at noon."

Guillermo took a deep breath and scratched the back of his head. He looked uneasily at her. Nonetheless, he agreed. Marisol would do the searches for ferry schedules, transportation, fares, sensations, pauses, laughter, and love. Before closing her agenda, she drew a red heart around August 29, 2012.

Chapter 2 – Missing

We have breaking news… Authorities activated an AMBER Alert after two teenagers were reported missing. Their names are Guillermo Pérez and Marisol Vargas, ages thirteen and twelve. Family members told authorities that neither returned home after school. The two are in the seventh grade at Emilio E. Huyke Junior High School in Río Piedras. They were last seen about six hours ago. We'd appreciate any information from our listeners that could possibly lead to their whereabouts.

This is Luis Ocasio, El Búho, reporting from your favorite radio station, WAPA-Radio 680 AM, always bringing you the latest news in Puerto Rico. The time: 7:35 p.m.

Chapter 3 - Demetrio, the Indian

The fortysomething Demetrio Mojica, a public transportation driver known by his friends as El Indio, had spent the last twenty-two years driving the same route from Fajardo to Río Piedras and back. He inherited both his grandfather's moniker and looks: swarthy, with brown, almond-shaped eyes and abundant dark hair tied back with a rubber band. September would mark his first anniversary living alone after his divorce. His taste for women had driven his marriage to the ground. Still, he loved spending time with his youngest daughter, even though he rarely got the chance to see her each month. Chloe, his ex-wife, knew he missed the girl, so she intentionally clung to the divorce settlement to make him miserable.

His visitation rights were stipulated and signed in black and white; Chloe was unyielding when he wanted to see the girl before or after the days agreed on. His eldest son was already grown and living on his own. Demetrio saw him every two years, perhaps, when he made enough to buy him a ticket from Florida to Puerto Rico. Even though the boy lived in the "richest nation in the world," his income as a mechanic wasn't enough for him to visit the island whenever he wished.

The night before the kids went missing, Demetrio was unable to sleep. He opened one eye and saw the blue neon light from his alarm clock on his nightstand.

Three in the morning. Dammit! Only eccentric artists are up at this hour.

Once again, insomnia had taken over. He struggled against his intruder for a few minutes, to no avail. The weight of his thoughts only multiplied. In frustration, he struck the bed with his fists and shot up seated on the left side, facing the sole window of the apartment he had been renting for the past year. A moonbeam shone on him, and he smiled.

"Shine on, silver moon," he softly sang to himself while peering out the window to the placid town square of Fajardo.

He lit his first cigarette. Nothing was stirring outside. Even the stray cats had grown tired of waiting for a hungry mouse to venture into the town's dumpster. From afar, he saw the trees in the town square swaying to the rhythmic tropical breeze. The winds from the Atlantic coupled with the windward breezes caused the soft gusts at night. Demetrio sought solace in the morning peace, sucked hard on his cigarette and exhaled the last puff of smoke. Another day like the one before awaited, full of traffic and people.

The woman El Indio was seeing a year ago, while he was married, was much younger. She was a regular passenger he picked up in Luquillo and left in Río Piedras. She was a nurse practitioner who was quite friendly with the other passengers. When she found out El Indio was married, she showed up at the bus terminal where he was waiting for his regular customers. There, in front of everyone, she made a scene yelling, shaking her fists, and crying. When he got to his home in Fajardo that afternoon, Demetrio found his clothes, shoes, and books in a heap outside. His wife got an anonymous tip that day and she, without thinking twice, dumped his belongings on the sidewalk. Even the loose pages containing his poems with notes he jotted down were scattered down the street. Despite his begging and pleading, she never again opened the door to him, except to let her daughter outside to see him on visiting days.

Chapter 4 - The Romantics

Tired of living by himself, Demetrio sought comfort in writing. He was grateful that his ex-wife hadn't destroyed his poetry books entirely, despite the chore of putting them back together. He believed they harbored the sheer essence of romance. He was also fascinated by the excessive realism in the daily paper. "The world has to end," he said in his spare time while leafing through, over and over again, the pages filled with so many ads, even in these financially challenged times. He was overwhelmed by society's abusive materialism. He called it an *overdose of dollars*.

He evaded loneliness by retreating each night to a corner of his memories and quenching his thirst with a six pack. After his sixth can of beer, he would become the self-proclaimed number one fan of the *Romantics*. Each evening at dusk he joined several other guys with the same ideology in a neighborhood bar or bodega to kill time amid drinks, bets and dominos. Then, slightly before midnight, like frat brothers, they each ended their soiree with an aspirin dissolved in a shot of rum to forget their past sorrows, usually summarized in a woman's name. El Indio was bound to that romantic idea that took him back in time to his adolescence, even if it was only in his memory, without time or constraints. Flirting, the game of seduction, the passion of two bodies exploring one another was the *leitmotif* of his sunsets.

He recalled that last Monday in April in the 1970s. He was just two weeks away from finishing his last semester in the seventh grade when his teacher, Miss Conde, decided to go into labor prematurely, and a substitute teacher had to be assigned. That baby was like a blessing from Heaven for

Demetrio because that was when he fell in love for the first time.

The din in his classroom, as his classmates awaited the new teacher, could be heard as far away as the basketball court outside. A few, short sudden raps on the desk with a wooden ruler commanded silence from the whole class. Nothing could be heard throughout the classroom, not even breathing, because everyone was holding their breath.

"Quiet! Everyone back to your seats. The class is about to start!" said the firm voice of a young, slender woman with long hair.

In a matter of seconds, all the students were seated. They seemed to be quietly examining the new teacher in full detail. She was wearing a light blue dress and a string of pearls that played up her hair. As strict as she seemed, she also had an air of calmness to her. Demetrio always believed she was sent to this Earth on a special mission. That scent of the sea embodying a woman became his very first anguish in love. Overwhelmed by his teenage hormones, he felt his pounding heart and thought he was about to have a heart attack. He would sweat heavily every time she was near. *I guess I'm going to die very young,* he'd think to himself, *I'm such an idiot.*

It was a poem by José de Diego *"A Laura,"* that left a mark on him, searingly branded on his skin. The substitute teacher would recite the poem with such passion, that he fell heavily in love with her. He loved her from afar. And he memorized the scent of her body until he was able to conjure it at will.

In his notebook filled with his poems, El Indio still kept that piece of paper folded in four containing his verses dedicated to his teacher. Moved by a passion, until then unbeknownst to him, he wrote a poem, at least each week, inspired by her. Each verse exuded his flesh, his soul, his heart.

He was rough and loved sports. But he quit playing basketball with his friends and locked himself in his room to write and rewrite poems dedicated to his teacher. He read them out loud, imitating her inflections when she recited poems in class. He mustered the courage to give her only one of his verses. Engraved in his memory was how his hands shook and his whole body flushed with heat when he handed her the folded and moist paper. She counted it as a bonus for his grades, never realizing Demetrio's true feelings for her. During summer vacation, he read "The little boy driven mad by love," and had his mother not realized that he was throwing away his food after playing with it on his plate, he would have starved to death.

His mad love came to an end when he started high school and met his first girlfriend: Veronica. Then came Esther, Susana, Nery, Carla, until he lost count of his many girlfriends and *special* friends. Poetry was his best ally in the art of seduction. El Indio recognized his weakness for women. So much so, that he sought help from his school counselor who referred him to a psychologist, who determined that his behavior was out of hand.

On the first day of class his senior year, his life took an unexpected turn: there was a new girl in school. Her name was Chloe and she was from New York. She was visiting the island with her parents—both Puerto Rican—who were closing a family business deal. Chloe didn't speak much, although she could understand everything when they spoke to her. She kept to herself not only because she was embarrassed by her American accent in Spanish, but also because her silent demeanor was a way of rebelling against her parents. Demetrio carefully observed her. He admired everything about her, even the way she carried her books, as if guarding all the universe's secrets. On the third day, Demetrio decided he couldn't take it anymore. He cut in the school cafeteria line and stood behind her. He polished up on his English with the help of the library's language audio tapes and he spent the entire walk to school practicing, in the manliest voice he could muster, a few words to introduce himself. He fixed his white shirt's collar and greeted her in English, the way he had practiced. She turned around and curtly, answered, "Don't even try it." He was left speechless, so mixed the two languages and created a new dialect. He took a deep breath and started anew, this time in Spanish:

"Oh, sorry. Oh my God! My name is Demetrio. What's yours?" he stuttered.

"Chloe," she said with a fake smile.

"Clo what? Sorry. My English isn't very good," replied Demetrio, now pale with his hands on his head.

"My name is Chloe and I understand Spanish," she said with a hint of resignation.

"Oh, what a relief!" said Demetrio, wiping his forehead with his sleeve. "You were making me sweat here."

"But please speak slowly because everyone talks so fast," she said, shifting her backpack to her right shoulder.

"Yeah, of course. No problem!" he said triumphantly, letting out a sigh. "Let me carry your backpack."

"I'm sorry, what?" said Chloe confused.

"Will you let me carry your backpack?" he said, pointing to her back.

"Oh, my backpack! No, thanks. I'm fine".

From that day on, Demetrio never left Chloe's side. He accompanied her to all her classes. He carried her books. He went with her to the lunchroom. And after a week, he started picking her up at her house in the morning to walk her to school, and in the afternoons, he walked her back home. From the door, her parents watched the puppy love romance blossom.

The new girl mesmerized him in every way, even more so when she started opening up to him and flirting with her bewitching eyes. He started writing a collection of poems on her; her beauty, her eyes, and he filled his poems with clichés that made him smile when he was alone. None of his previous girlfriends compared to her. Chloe had a mature attitude, seldom seen in girls her age. Her elegant and measured gait captured the attention from both men and women. Demetrio compared her to an orchid, delicate in form and color, and considered her an ethereal being. He thought that she possessed a quality far superior than that of poetry; all he had to do was merely think of standing close to her and his voice broke. At last, El Indio had found love. He told his friends about that special something that caused butterflies in his stomach and reached every part of his body. His friends thought he was crazy! Amid chuckles he told them how his heart beats so quickly and how he could spend hours thinking only about her. In other words, Demetrio had been transformed by the very same sentimentality that he swore he would never feel again after almost going crazy for the seventh-grade substitute teacher. Chloe liked the attention she was getting from him and allowed him to carry her backpack each day to her doorstep.

Throughout the whole school, word spread about Demetrio and *la gringuita,* as his ex-girlfriends called her. When the two walked by the science classroom holding hands, the other girls fumed with envy and did everything possible to draw his attention.

"He never looked at me *that* way," said Esther, twirling a lollipop between her pouty lips.

"In what way?" asked one of her friends.

"Didn't you see him? With that idiotic face and the haughtiness of *Pepe Le Pew*!"

"The idiot looks damn fine!"

"Shut up! We have to think of something," said the glassy eyed Esther.

"What are you up to, bitch?"

"Nothing. Just get the gang together during recess. I have a plan," she said chewing on the remains of a lollipop now turned into gum.

The school bell rang at noon. Demetrio was the first to exit the chemistry lab to meet Chloe under the *ceiba* tree between the school's two buildings. He was pushing his way through the students, uttering *excuse me* along the way.

He moved cautiously, carefully maneuvering his way between the other kids, attempting to avoid touching them. He only felt worthy of being touched by Chloe.

He was coming out of the north building and was already walking on the lawn when he saw that Chloe was not there. She had never failed him. She usually waited for him there, sitting on the roots surrounding the tree that looked like rustic table legs. He came to a quick halt with his hands on his waist. He broke into a sly smile. He ran around the tree, believing she was playing hide-and-seek. But she wasn't. He scratched his head in disbelief. He heard the clamor of laughter. They were coming from one of the classrooms in the southern building. Glancing toward the building, he saw a bunch of girls, looking out the window like an eight-headed dragon, and laughing loud and hard.

"What happened, Dimitri? Did you lose your *gringuita?*" said a familiar female voice.

They're up to something, thought Demetrio. *And I'll found out what it is.*

"Hey, girls! Have you seen Chloe?"

Some of them replied *yes* and others replied *no.*

"What happened? Did you lose her? Maybe she went back to New York!" yelled Esther, who started laughing hysterically, while the others joined her in chorus.

Demetrio started walking toward the classroom and the girls all ran out screaming and hiding.

I wonder what happened to Chloe? If she was leaving early, she would have told me, he thought.

He didn't know what to do. He only had half an hour left for his lunch break, so he headed sulking toward the lunchroom. He instinctively picked up the green tray and stood in the longest line he had ever seen in all his years at school. He observed the people in line, hoping to see her, but there was no one with her abundant hair tied in a ponytail and her sun-kissed complexion. He was lost in thought until someone from one of the tables shouted: "Hey Indio, asshole, move it!" He looked back. They were yelling at him.

Demetrio held up two fingers in a peace sign, and one of the boys at the table retorted by holding up his middle finger. Everyone was laughing. El Indio felt a bolt of hot lightening shooting up from his feet to his chest. With his eyes spewing fire, he left the line and went straight to the school bullies at the table. They called themselves *Los Pileñetas.* At their leader's orders, they all stood up, puffed their chests and, grabbing glasses full of chocolate milk, were ready to fight. Demetrio slowed down. One of the lunchroom workers, with her hair in a net, was at that moment serving papaya chunks in syrup when she saw the scene. She pictured herself cleaning up the lunchroom after a food fight. "Hey, all of you! What's going on over there? You guys!" yelled the employee, letting go of the serving spoon and warning: "Look who's on his way! It's the principal!"

One of the lunchroom employees walked briskly to the table. She looked at Demetrio and pointed to the door. She managed to calm down the novice delinquents with a few mint candies she pulled out from her apron.

Demetrio rushed out of the lunchroom with his shirt soaked in sweat. His classmates greeted him as he passed by, but he could neither see nor hear them. Every cell in his body was red hot, focusing on only one person: Chloe. He went back to the tree and stood between two statues that were diverting the asymmetrical trunk from its roots. From his back pants pocket he pulled a folded piece of paper and read what he had written in the previous class: "You are the most beautiful and precious thing I have. I wouldn't mind losing all my possessions because nothing compares to the richness of your spirit. The beauty and love you offer me fill the coffer of my soul." A dark silence was growing inside him. His eyes welled with tears and he blinked several times to keep a tear from falling. The sound of the school bell signaling the end of the lunch period brought him back to reality, and the school chatter grew louder as droves of students returned to their classes. El Indio, cocooned by the tree, lifted his head and rushed away.

Demetrio approached Don Tino, the school janitor who was coiling around a chain from the entrance gate.

"How are you Don Tino? Please don't close the gate yet. I have to leave."

"Says who?" asked the janitor automatically, without even turning around to see who was talking.

"Well, my girl got out early, you know..." he replied worried.

He then turned around and saw Demetrio.

"Well, look who's here! El Indio! Oh, yes. That's right." Don Tino spoke slowly, taking his time to find his words. "She left at around ten this morning. I opened the gate for her."

"Do you know why?" asked Demetrio immediately, suddenly waking from the stupor that had been enveloping him for nearly an hour.

"Erm, well, you see…Geez, I don't remember!" said the man while scratching his head.

"Please Don Tino, make an effort! Was she sick? Was she crying? Did she leave with someone?"

"Erm, I guess not."

"You guess not what?" asked Demetrio, grabbing the janitor's arm.

"She was alone. Yes, she had an excuse from the office."

"And what did it say?"

"Oh, I have no idea."

"But Don Tino, that's what the excuse is for! Oh, geez!" said Demetrio, clenching his hands.

"Look, son, you'd better be on your way. I gotta clean the bathrooms now."

Demetrio was by himself on the sidewalk and, without thinking twice, he quickly traced the path that for months he had been taking alongside Chloe. It was at that moment that he took a good look at his surroundings and realized that the building on the corner had been painted yellow, that there was a new florist's shop across the street, that on the other side there was a *criollo* hot dog cart, that the González Pharmacy was now Moscoso Pharmacy, and that the antiques shop had *For Sale* written in huge white letters all over its storefront windows. Demetrio scratched his ear and looked at everything as if seeing for the first time, so many changes at once. He walked along the main street. He pushed his way through so many people; some coming, others going, elderly women with bags of groceries, men dressed almost identically in dark pants and white shirts, and children hanging on to their mothers' skirts. From afar, he saw the line of parked public vans. Searching his pocket, he pulled out thirty-five cents to pay the car fare. He then approached the drivers standing in front of the cars.

"Is there room for one more?" asked Demetrio.

"Sure. We leave in about five minutes," replied the driver with the cigarette dangling from his mouth.

Inside the van, Demetrio felt the heat of a roast oven. The odor of freshly chopped onions and cheap cologne hit his nostrils. In the front row next to the driver sat a dark-skinned woman who soaked up the sweat from her face with a wrinkled handkerchief. Sitting in the row behind her were two fifty-something men. When they saw him they sat farther apart and spread their legs wider, leaving no room for him. Behind them sat a female college student peering out the window into the distance. The other passengers watched in disgust how, from her mouth, she stretched chewing gum into a string and wrapped it around her finger. She repeated this procedure over and over: she would push the gum back into her mouth, chomp on it, squeeze it between teeth, stretch it with her finger like a rubber band and, before it could snap, she would push it into her mouth again. She had no idea she was being watched by the men in the van. And seated in the rear of the van—in the kitchen, as they called it—was a mother with her two children, one on each side. As they waited, the passengers fanned themselves with whatever they had available: fans, handkerchiefs, envelopes, notebooks. El Indio sat in the second row and left plenty of space between himself and the college girl. His was one of the first stops.

After exactly five minutes, as he promised, the driver took his last puff before closing the van's two doors. He walked in front of the van to the driver's side and pulled out from his pocket a key attached to a tiny jet hand. He then heaved into the crumbled and deformed leather seat, its coils squeaking under his weight. He turned the ignition on and, without uttering a word, stepped on the pedal. Another driver with the right of way abruptly stopped before hitting him and honked his horn. He almost fell out of the car window insulting the other public van driver.

"Sup? Why drive so slow? C'mon!" said the driver, ignoring the honking and waving of fists.

The driver eased into the right lane as close as possible to the road leading into the residential areas and housing projects. The passengers' faces displayed relief. At last, they were on their way. Demetrio, meanwhile, was on his way to a change in his life; kismet awaited.

He was the first to hop out of the van. On his way to Chloe's house, he walked three blocks and turned right on *Valparaíso* Street. The busy buzz of the city was now in the background. Demetrio was nervous, anxious over finding out what happened to his girlfriend. The intense one o'clock sun prompted him to go slower.

A Labrador-German shepherd mix, tied to the gate of a dilapidated home, heard Demetrio's steps as they quickened. The dog started barking in a frenzy, as if warning the neighborhood that an intruder was approaching. Demetrio was familiar with the dog and whistled at him. Slowly, he got closer.

"Hi, cutie! Easy, it's me. Have you seen Chloe?"

The dog zealously wagged its tail and let the teenager pet its head. He sniffed and licked the boy's hand.

The next home was Chloe's. It was all closed, including its glass kitchen windows. He peered through the window, attempting to make out a human form. He saw nothing. He tapped on the wooden door, now weathered by the rain. He waited a few seconds and tried again.

"Chloe, are you there?" he said softly.

He felt weak from the day's heat and a missed lunch. He leaned his head against the door and called her name again, but this time in a near whisper.

"Chloe, my love, where are you?"

He then heard someone approaching the door from the inside of the home. He heard the door being unlocked. Her face appeared. Her eyes looked sunken and her face showed traces of sorrow.

"What are you doing here?" she asked, still dressed in her school uniform, but barefoot.

"I'm asking the same question," said Demetrio, shrugging.

She didn't answer and remained still at the door.

"Chloe, what's wrong? May I come in? Could I have some water?"

"My folks aren't here."

"So? I've been here before when they weren't around. Why can't I come in now?" asked Demetrio wondering why she was so cold.

He leaned forward to give her a kiss, but she brushed him away.

"Not now."

"C'mon Chloe, please tell me! You're making me miserable!"

"I'm making you miserable?"

"Really! Tell me what's wrong. Please let me in!" he pleaded, searching her eyes.

She opened the door and headed toward the kitchen. Demetrio followed behind and pulled a chair from the pinewood dining table. He sat on it. He shooed away several fruit flies from the fruit basket on the table. He then grabbed a banana, but seeing how mushy it was, he put it back in the basket. As he wiped his hands on his pants, he was fascinated by how softly Chloe pushed herself on her tip-toes to reach a greenish glass stamped with the Coca-Cola brand. She went to the refrigerator and poured water with a lemony fragrance from a pitcher. Demetrio waited in silence with his arms crossed, his legs twitching nervously. Chloe served him water, and he was even more surprised at her aloofness. The heat and the anticipation made him anxious. Chloe pulled a wrinkled piece of paper from the pocket of her blue plaid skirt.

"I got this in my social studies class."

"Who gave it to you? What does it say?" asked Demetrio.

"It was on my desk. It's a love letter for Esther…from YOU!" she yelled, throwing the paper in his face.

"What?? But…" and then he picked it up from the floor. "This isn't mine. No wonder!"

"No wonder what?" she said, with her hands on her waist.

"It's just that the girls, you know, Esther and her friends…How do I explain it…Look, when I got to the tree and didn't see you, they started taunting me and laughing from one of the classrooms."

Chloe remained silent and Demetrio remained agitated.

"Now I get it! They were lying. It was a trap; I swear it was!"

"Are you sure?" she asked.

"I swear to God Almighty!" he said, with his posture as if pledging an oath.

"I was hurt, you know! And one more thing, Demetrio Mojica…I will never, ever forgive unfatefulness from you!" she said furrowing her brow.

"You mean unfaithfulness."

"Yeah, that."

Demetrio swore a thousand times he did not write that letter; even though they tried to fake his handwriting, the letter was poorly written. He pulled from his back pants pocket the poem he wrote that morning and showed it to her.

"You see? This is my handwriting. Go on, read it. It's for you."

The two were now calmer. Chloe took the piece of paper and read very intently the poem she inspired. She sighed and looked at him. She was different now. He was still concerned, but something had changed in him as well. He opened his arms to Chloe and said with urgency:

"Come to me! What more proof do you want?"

They embraced and he gently pulled up her chin and kissed her, like the first time, with a brush on the lips.

"May I say something to you," she asked, pulling away.

"Sure."

"You stink to high heaven," she said chuckling. "*Mami* won't get here until later. You can shower here if you want."

He sniffed his left armpit and muttered quite frankly:

"Geez!" And then he lifted his arms as if he were a ferocious wolf, and in a roaring voice yelled: "Take me my little red riding hood!"

Chloe gave him a mischievous, yet timid glance and, taking him by the hand, she guided him to the bathroom. She handed him a towel and closed the door.

El Indio immediately sensed the game she was inviting him to play. He felt a warmth in his chest that traveled down between his legs. With cold water beating on his face, he closed his eyes for a few seconds and welcomed the water as a true symbol of baptism, of an initiation. An initiation to pleasure. An initiation into the essence of a woman; the essence of consensual ecstasy. He wasn't thinking clearly. Actually, he didn't want reason to get in the way of passion.

She was sixteen; he had just turned seventeen. Demetrio was a virgin and the chance for pleasure had arrived unannounced. By the time he finished showering and exited the bathroom, he was visibly aroused; and she was waiting by her bedroom, wrapped in a towel with a daisy print. The daisies highlighted her breasts and he, covering his genitals with his hands, could not take his eyes off them. Chloe took him by the hand, still holding the towel with her other hand, and led him to the bed. Throughout the forty-eight seconds they were seated on the edge of the bed, they played at holding hands and interlacing their fingers, giggling nervously. Even though Demetrio had seen pictures of naked women, the mere thought of having a real one right there was a chance he could not waste, much less with the woman who was his true love.

She was familiar with foreplay, but she knew when to be bashful, so she let Demetrio take the lead. After a few seconds of silence, Chloe grabbed her biology textbook, which she had casually placed on the pillow to show him a few *interesting* pictures on human reproduction. She leafed through the book, unable to find what she was looking for. El Indio brushed the tips of his fingers on the cotton sheets and caressed her thigh. He looked at her, waiting for a response. She drew closer and knelt on the bed. Demetrio did the same and, surrounding her waist with his arms, kissed her, their nude torsos in complete contact. Chloe wrapped her arms around his neck, pulled him closer to her breasts and their tongues met. He was unable to contain himself and ejaculated. He got off from the bed in frustration. Chloe followed him to the bathroom, but El Indio turned around and asked her to wait in the room. "I'll be on the bed," she told him.

While wiping himself he anxiously thought: *Don't be such an idiot.* He washed his hands with plenty of soap, looked in the mirror and slapped himself. He then smoothed his wet hair behind his ears. He took a deep breath and then came out.

"I found the pages I was looking for," she said when she saw him.

Demetrio went into the bedroom and closed the door behind him. She invited him to the bed. He leafed through the book feigning interest; Chloe brushed her finger down his back, starting at his shoulders and ending at his buttocks. To keep the desire going, she then tried it with her lips. El Indio tossed the book aside and turned around. She, anxious to be fully naked, slowly removed her towel from around her waist and remained still, ready to receive the awaited caresses. He had not yet placed a finger on her and already she was feeling a tingling sensation from her navel to her groin.

Demetrio brushed his wet fingers against her lips. She closed her eyes. He was discovering the sensuousness of the female body and strummed her skin with his fingers. He caressed her slowly. He cupped her breasts and kissed them, discovering new sensations behind her eyelids. With his finger, he slowly drew circles on her soft belly, like a curious child. He continued, touching from head to toe: her mouth, neck, shoulders, breasts, hips, thighs, and then he remained confined to her hidden folds. Demetrio's calmness turned into frenzied desire and wished that all time would stand still. There was no room for time, no room for hours or minutes. And now, engaged in sheer pleasure, they moaned until their throats were parched. Chloe begged with her eyes. He then felt a primitive desire to couple his sexuality with hers. It was three o'clock. On the other side of town, the school bell was ringing.

El Indio was feeling so manly, ready again for another life-giving eruption. He held back. He doused heavily in sweat. He surrounded her waist with his arms, but he couldn't decide whether to go up or down. She guided his hand and showed him the way. Arching her back, Chloe surrendered to her fantasies. He sensed a new aroma to her. She suddenly shot up and pushed Demetrio on his back to the bed. He was surprised, but he followed her lead. El Indio would never forget how Chloe was on top in attentive command. In his eyes, she had become an Amazon warrior mounting rhythmically, skillfully like no other, willing to carry out an unparalleled sacrifice.

Chloe was filled with a life-giving force. But nine months later, she would be a completely different person.

Chapter 5 - *¡Ay Bendito! Oh, bless you!*

"What a damn shame!" said the women in the neighborhood when they heard of Chloe's pregnancy.

For Demetrio's mother and the nearby wagging tongues, Demetrio's future was now on hold.

"*Ay bendito!*" they said. "Kiss college good-bye. Forget about becoming a doctor, or a lawyer, or an engineer."

A few of the women in the neighborhood who, *by mere coincidence*, were all on the sidewalk taking out the garbage concurred that the couple's honeymoon phase would be over within a year. One of them, with her hair in rollers, said the teen marriage would not last. No one contradicted her. All were certain the couple's new life together would unfold like a Mexican *telenovela* in all its drama.

Not even Demetrio's grandmother was able to come to his aid, despite lighting a candle to the Virgin of the Miracles and praying the rosary out loud. In fact, no one really desired to help Demetrio, now debuting as a father before having the chance of living a bachelor's life.

On the positive side, gossiping about the young couple would keep the neighborhood united until something newer happened.

In another suburban neighborhood, Chloe's father swore over the trouble his only daughter was in, blaming his wife and the lack of responsibility from the future father's family.

"Ok, I'm done with the memories!" growled Demetrio through his teeth, chugging down his sixth can of beer, smacking the table in frustration.

The sound of his hand hitting the wood was magnified by the ring in the form of an Indian head he wore on his right pinkie. The ring was a gift from his grandmother for giving her the first great-grandchild—a boy, no less. It was for good luck, she said. He still remembered the words from the woman he considered so wise: "Everyone brings gifts to the baby, but they forget about the poor father."

The loneliness in his rented room and the old family photograph in it made him yearn for the family life he once had. Chloe never forgave the only act of infidelity she found out about; he had cheated a few times, but she only found out about one. Demetrio lost hope in love, although he knew that sooner or later, he would be the antagonist in an unfortunate story. He knew the stakes were high, so he gambled and lost. His taste for women had been, and still was, his weakness. He recalled when the school counselor told him he had no shame. He was aware of it: his true love had been Chloe, but that was over. He was now trying to make amends through WA— Womanizers' Anonymous—a group that met frequently to drink rum and play dominoes. But on those sleepless nights, only Chloe filled his memories.

Oh, my dear Chloe! How can I forget our first time together that afternoon? You were so beautiful. But it is my fault it all ended. Why do I fancy women so much? And what about love? Does it really exist or is it merely something invented by society? Is love for real? Oh, but women are delicious! Indeed, they are. But the younger ones don't even look at me anymore, only horny old ladies who are running out of time. The irony is that I'm still strong, like a wild bull, as my grandmother used to say. I still have a full head of hair, maybe with some gray. Nowadays, people are more infatuated than in love. What was that saying, that only a parent gives unconditional love? But youth doesn't heed sayings, does it?

In my case, it was bad luck. Or maybe it was good luck. "You sure hit the bullseye the first time," said my grandmother. Oh, abuela, are you watching over me from up above, as you promised you would? I don't think so.

Chapter 6 - The Firstborn

His cell phone alarm pulled him back to the present moment. It was 5 a.m. He was on his second *cortado*, no sugar. At his age, Demetrio felt the effects of caffeine right smack in his heart. When the throbbing came, he'd shimmy his shoulders, as if shaking off an evil spirit. He laughed inwardly, remembering how his son, at the age of four, imitated him.

The memories kept flowing as he got ready for work. His first son was born on the same day he graduated from high school. Looking back, El Indio recalled the day when his plans for a degree in Literature came to a screeching halt. Not even enrolling in college was on the horizon. Demetrio was starting a family and all his friends congratulated him. But inside, he felt helpless.

They named the baby Carlos in honor of the governor at the time—Carlos Romero Barceló. Chloe's parents chose the name in gracious return for a helping hand from *La Fortaleza* in boosting their business in Puerto Rico. Demetrio always wondered what kind of business Chloe's father ran. He was never welcomed to participate, much less after ruining the career in politics Chloe's father had planned for her.

All for the better, he thought to himself while blowing the coffee to cool it down.

The day Carlos was born seemed to never end. "Had there been cell phones then, I would have gotten to the hospital on time," Demetrio mused while fidgeting with his phone.

Chloe had complained of a backache the night before. Her mother, intuitively knowing what was to come, lent

Demetrio her car so that he could come directly home after the lengthy commencement ceremony.

That very same afternoon, he received several invitations to after-graduation parties from different school cliques: from the *salseros*, the rock and rollers, the Future Housewives of America, the Catholics, the Protestants, the Business Administration group and even the feared *Pileñetas*. All would have a *close encounter* in a discotheque shaped like a flying saucer in Isla Verde. A doleful Demetrio had to turn them all down.

When he returned home—actually, it was Chloe's parents' home, where he lived after news of the pregnancy—he found a note on the dining table that read: "In labor."

He immediately went to pick up his mother and grandmother. But his mother had to make several stops on the way to the hospital.

"But *Mami*, we have no time!" he said anxiously.

"*Mijo*, we can't just go there empty handed. And hurry up, you're too slow," said his mother as she glanced in the mirror and smoothed her hair.

"I don't have any money!" he said.

"Don't worry, *mijo*," said his grandmother, "Thank God I got my Social Security check this week. It's not much, but it'll do," she said, clutching her worn pocketbook.

They arrived at the hospital and entered through the Emergency Ward, where they were told how to go to the waiting room. Demetrio went straight to the counter.

"I'm looking for Chloe Mojica," he said.

"How do you spell it?"

"C-h-l-o-e," replied the teen, with a sobriety that surprised even him.

"Nope, nobody here by that name," said the receptionist.

"*Mijo*, she goes by her maiden last names," said the grandmother, giving him a slight smack on the shoulder with her fan.

"Naranjo. Yes, her name is Chloe Naranjo Barceló," said El Indio, as if guessing the answer to difficult question.

"Oh, she must be related to the governor," mumbled the woman. "Yes, here she is. Second floor, room 208. But wait a minute, young man. These are not visiting hours. You'll have to wait until five."

He looked at the floor. His mother pushed him aside.

"*Ay bendito*, ma'am, the mother is waiting for him to dress the baby. He was born premature at seven months. Look, I have the bag with his clothes here," said Demetrio's mother, lifting the bag of baby clothes for all to see.

"In that case, only *he* is allowed to go up. You two ladies have to remain seated here," she said.

"Thanks," said Demetrio, with waning enthusiasm.

Coming out of the elevator was Roque, an old family neighbor. The neighbors nicknamed him "Screw" because he was a mechanic and each week he parked a new car in front of his house. The two were surprised to see each other there.

"El Indio! What are you doing here, boy?"

"Well, my girlfriend had a baby."

"Well, surprise, surprise…Look, son, do you need a job, now that you're a dad?" said Roque with a dash of sarcasm.

While searching Demetrio's face, Roque pulled a cigarette from behind his ear, placed it between his lips and patted his pockets in search of a lighter.

"I guess so," said the teen who was caught off guard by the question.

Roque simply smiled with the unlit cigarette in his mouth. He outstretched his hand for a *gimme five*.

"Let's have a five, brother. Have a cigarette and my card. Give me a call. I think I might have something for you. And congratulations, *Papá.*"

Roque left the elevator and walked down the corridor in a peculiar way: with his left foot in a lilt, as if he had a spring in his knee. Demetrio pressed the second-floor button. When the two doors closed, he felt chills and cowered in a corner with his arms folded and his head hanging, almost reaching his chest.

As soon as the elevator began to lift, he felt overwhelmed until it reached the second floor for *penitent women*, which is how his family described women in labor. As the doors opened, he whiffed disinfectant, medicine and alcohol. He exited the elevator in fear. To the right were two steel doors with small windows and a sign that read: Authorized Personnel. Just out of curiosity, he peered through the glass. Nothing caught his eye. He slowly headed in the opposite direction toward the Operating Room. His legs were heavy, and he had no desire to reach Room 208. He heard a soft wailing in a feminine voice followed by sobbing. He turned left and found a group of nurses attentively listening to another one who stood out because she was wearing a cap in the shape of a paper boat. One of the nurses saw him walking by, and he quickened his pace. He continued down to the end of the corridor and was startled upon hearing a dissonant voice blaring from the ceiling: "Doctor Ortiz, you are needed in the delivery room, Doctor Ortiz…" The voice over the loudspeaker vanished from Demetrio's head when he spotted the room number he was looking for.

He gently pushed the door that was ajar and froze when he saw Chloe so helpless on the bed.

What have I done to you! he thought.

Her parents were with her. Her mother, on a seat in a corner, was wearing a sweater far too warm for the tropics. It was cold in the hospital, though. While she leafed through a gossip magazine, the father was peering out the window.

Chloe, half asleep, opened her eyes and looked at the door. She smiled and he smiled back. A nervous Demetrio clumsily moved his hand and dissipated all silence in the room by dropping the bag containing the baby's clothes. He quickly picked it up.

"Well look what the cat dragged in!" said Chloe's father who glanced at the mother, opened his eyes, and grimaced in disapproval.

"Good afternoon," said a cornered Demetrio. His greeting was met with silence. After three long seconds, Chloe's mother looked at her watch and, without lifting her eyes from the magazine, asked, "How was the ceremony?"

"The what?"

"The commencement ceremony, son, how was it?" she insisted.

"It was okay," he answered. He walked to his girlfriend, took her hand and mumbled: "How are you?"

"Not too well. I'm in pain…" uttered her dry lips in a childish voice.

Her mother rushed in, "What hurts, sweetie? What do you need? Shall I call the nurse?"

The girl closed her eyes. The father interpreted his daughter's expression and said: "Woman, I'm a bit hungry. Let's go to the cafeteria."

He looked at his daughter and asked, "Baby, do you want something?"

"No Daddy, thank you."

Chloe's mother gently caressed her daughter's head, as if she were a little girl again. She grabbed her bag and left the room. Demetrio stood motionless by the metal rod sustaining the IV fluid. He sighed in relief when Chloe's parents left. The girl tapped the bed, motioning for him to sit. He did so with extreme care, making sure not to cause her more pain.

Chapter 7 - The Morning Ritual

It was 5:30 a.m. His second morning alarm went off and pulled Demetrio out of his nostalgic stupor. He looked at his hands. They were dry.

I've been a public van driver since I was young. Look at how this job has wrung me dry, he thought.

He gulped down the rest of his coffee and got up to start his day. He grabbed his van key and the pocket notebook for jotting down an idea or a nice phrase that might come to mind. He went down the stairs, two steps at a time, and once out of the old boarding home, he swiped the first newspaper from the packet of freshly printed copies deposited by the entrance of Funerary Mercado. With his head high, he crossed the street to the Fajardo town square and, in his usual morning routine, he bowed his head before the statue of the statesman.

"Puerto Rico above all," he uttered, repeating the quote at the foot of the statue of Antonio R. Barceló.

El Indio then made his way briskly down the street of the square; he passed behind the church and made the sign of the cross, and then made an X sign with his two index fingers when passing in front of the military apparel store on the corner. Demetrio disliked the armed forces. His childhood was marked by the commotion, the wailing and sobbing by his mother and grandmother when they read the letter that said his father had died in the Korean war. Since then, he equated all things military with tragedy.

"In the name of the Father, the Son, the Holy Church and the Military. Oh, the divine irony!" He made the signed of the cross again and slowed down his pace.

He saw a shadow in one of the alleyways. He walked slowly, observing all the dark corners of the nearby streets connecting with the main avenue. There was no one. He continued down the street, quickening his pace. In less than two minutes he was already in the newly remodeled public terminal of the town of Fajardo.

"It's going to be a good day, right? Maybe not!" he said, lighting another cigarette.

"Talking to yourself again?" said another driver behind him.

"None of your business."

The other driver continued on his way, laughing and gesturing crazy with his finger.
Demetrio ignored him and walked to the end of the second row of parked vans to where his vehicle was. He opened all the doors and cleaned the inside with a battery powered vacuum cleaner he kept in the back of the van. He went on to clean the windshields and windows, wiping away the finger marks left by the passengers of the previous day. He spritzed the inside of the van with a piña colada fragrance and tapped the tiny braless hula dancer on the dashboard.

His cell phone had another ringtone this time: a horse neighing. He turned it off. He hurriedly wiped down the van's chassis with a dry towel and closed each door, except for the passenger door. He whistled at the man in charge of the public station and signaled for him to look after his van. The man, yawning, nodded he would. Demetrio felt his back pocket and headed toward Mollie's Café. He was mumbling an old song: *Sombras nada más*. He entered the café and took a deep breath, inhaling the aroma of freshly baked bread and freshly brewed coffee.

"Good morning, beautiful!" he said, smiling at Elena, the employee in the shift. "The usual."

"A *medianoche* with black coffee for El Indio," yelled the woman, who then lowered her voice and said: "Uh, I saw you talking to yourself this morning."

"Really? Where?"

"By the statue on the square. One of these days the statue is going to answer and scare you out of your wits," said the woman laughing and covering her mouth with her hand to hide her missing teeth.

"But *mija*, don't you know that it already said something to me?"

"Oh yeah, and what did it say?"

"That there's a woman with missing teeth who's in love with me."

"You rascal, you! If my husband catches you…!"

"But who said it was you?" added Demetrio, and he paid for his breakfast.

"You clown!" she said annoyed and handed him his change along with a receipt printed with the *lotto tax* numbers.

"You can throw the receipt away. That's the government for you, adding more taxes and tricking people with an imaginary lotto on the taxes. I know better!"

As he waited for his breakfast, he glanced at the first few pages of the newspaper and was disturbed by a headline: "Another Girl Disappears in Vieques."

My God, that's more than three already! he thought, and he pulled out his wallet where he kept a picture of his two children.

Chapter 8 - El Cadi and La Biz

The morning sun was already warming the sea breeze in Vieques, where slight gusts along the shore carried with them particles of sand and sea. The sun's rays relentlessly pierced the small island's foliage and dressed the homes on the eastern portion with light. To the west, the cloak of nocturnal haze on the sandy ground was vanishing like a ghost. Further into the horizon, in a pinpoint of light, a fisherman was sailing into the infinite blue.

While Demetrio sat in Fajardo reading about the disappearance of another girl, El Cadi was in Vieques reading the same story. After showering that morning, El Cadi wrapped a white towel around his freckled hips and grabbed a beer from the refrigerator. He knew he would find the anticipated story in the paper, so he settled in his chair and placed the bottle of beer in the round hole on the chairs' arm. For the sake of purity, he preferred all things white, a color his mother also liked because it soothed her. Everything surrounding him was white: the floor, the walls, the curtains, the rug, the dishes, the appliances. He believed, he had inherited this fixation.

Before opening the paper, he sighed in satisfaction and peered through the open window, losing his attention in the emerging scenery. The sun was making its broad entrance, slowly illuminating the night's impermanence. The quietness in La Hueca was interrupted by a few roaming kingbirds dodging the sudden gusts from the trade winds that suddenly shook the branches in the tallest tress. El Cadi was still as captivated by the tropical beauty of Vieques—Isla Nena, as it was nicknamed—as he was the first time he arrived as a teenager, with no idea whatsoever that he would stay for good.

He returned to the paper. Upon seeing the picture of the girl, he licked his index finger and placed it on the girl's paper lips. He vigorously rubbed the image until dissolving it.

With total indifference, he licked his finger again to turn the page. Another headline caught his attention even more: ***The New Puerto Rican Diaspora***. He sat back in his chair and thought to himself: "Why would anyone leave this paradise."

Two nights earlier, El Cadi had remained awake until dawn, gagging his victim: a girl from Vieques who had been at the Blue Moon bar. A girl gang, that called itself *Las Biz* thought the bar was a strategic location for preying on rich boys who arrived with their family on fancy boats from Marina del Rey, in Fajardo.

The girl was a semester away from graduating high school in Vieques and was planning on leaving the island, as most kids did, after finishing school. Her father was a fisherman, and her mother was dying of cancer, which those close to her believed was caused by the hazardous wastes left behind by the U.S. Navy after their military practices were over on the island. The girl was upset over her life. She thought that she, a teenager, deserved more forms of entertainment than the small island had to offer. She wasn't settling for the alleged peace Vieques was now enjoying; she was bored. She dreamed about becoming a model and participating in one of those reality shows in the United States, where she would proclaim her pride in being a Boricua.

That night would be her initiation into *Las Biz*, an event that would pull her out of tedium and help her attain popularity in school. Her assignment was to ensnare a *zángano,* —worker bee— which was how the gang called any guy willing to leave with one of them at the slightest signal. The initiation rite included bringing before the other members a condom with the chosen guy's semen. The girl was a bit scared, but at the same time, excited. A rush of adrenaline kept her amused as she dressed for the event.

El Cadi was a regular at the Blue Moon. He didn't talk much and was always by himself. He worked in the family business of renting jeeps. He came and went as he pleased, and no one minded. He was twenty-eight and content with showing up at his father's office and then going for a cursory inspection of the vehicles. Putting in a couple of hours a day was enough to justify his salary. He then would vanish in his white jeep and was not seen in public again until supper time.

He arrived at the Blue Moon always at 8 p.m. sharp. He looked like a foreign secret agent as he made his way to the bar among the other customers in his usual deliberate and somber manner. The bar was devoid of all fanciness: only a few small round tables with battery lit candles. In the back, several green and blue neon lights lit the multiple liquor bottles. Against that backdrop, each of the customers at the bar seemed to be draining, drop by drop, into a single spirit.

The left corner of the bar was reserved for El Cadi. The owner kept his chair in a small closet and a waiter would pull it out minutes before he arrived. He would disinfect it and place it in the corner, just as El Cadi had ordered. The barman called him *el socio*—the partner—because of his generous tips and his loyalty to the place. The owner of the bar watched him through the tinted windows in his office on the second floor.

He went down to the bar with the excuse of asking for a Coke. But, he actually wanted to say hello to El Cadi and lay down the law so he'd know he was being watched. The owner then climbed up to his office again to keep an eye on anything suspicious.

That guy's weird. I wonder what he's hiding behind those shades, the owner would say to himself whenever he saw El Cadi with his aviator Ray-Bans, even at night.

El Cadi was rarely seen around the island, only in the scant hours he put in at his father's business. Mr. Richard was a widower when he moved to Vieques with his son fourteen years ago, along with a container he did not allow anyone to unload from the cargo ferry.

"Another outsider moves to paradise," said the neighbors, already accustomed to the diverse collection of foreigners that either put up a business or a summer home in Vieques.

El Cadi looked exactly like his father with caramel-colored eyes, abundant auburn hair, and thousands of freckles all over his almost six-foot tall frame. The somberness was etched in both their faces. They looked like descendants of an ancient Nordic tribe. *The Vikings,* that's how the locals called them behind their backs.

Richard Roldan III, aka El Cadi. What a name for a guy like that. Why the hell did that man move here on this tiny island with his son? And why does his name have a number in it? And if he's Richard III, then who's Richard II? Why wasn't there a woman with them, mused the bar owner until his cell phone interrupted his silent interrogation.

☼

It had been a normal, ordinary day for El Cadi the night the girl went missing. If something deviated from his plans, he would break out in hives all over his neck, arms and thighs. He would become upset to the extent of spending hours locked in the bathroom, talking into the mirrors until he calmed down.

Seated in his usual corner at the bar, he ordered his usual meal: a rare *churrasco* steak with fries. It was 11 p.m. He had been sitting for hours in the same spot. He was ordering another whiskey when she entered and glanced over the bar. She seemed to be looking for someone. She approached one of the waiters and he answered by shaking his head. The waiter led her to a table for two. She refused and pointed to an empty space at the end of the bar. Annoyed, the waiter shrugged his shoulders and turned to assist another customer.

The girl pressed her shiny clutch against her abdomen and sighed. She recalled an incredible story that one of the Las Biz girls told her about the Blue Moon's bar. The girl said that it was covered in scales from some sort of animal and that it harbored a sinister secret. The bar had a curved shape, much like a boa constrictor, and it was four meters long. Some said the owner had brought a boa constrictor from Brazil and had fattened it by feeding it his dead enemies. Others said that when he found out his young wife had been cheating on him—with another woman—he fed her and her lover to the boa. His wife and her lover had been missing for eight months and the police had no clues over their disappearance. They couldn't even find the dreaded animal.

The girl was wearing a tight, red dress that evening. Not a wrinkle was out of place along the contours of her near perfect figure. While making her way through the tables, the glances of envy and lust warmed her skin. Her high heels—

they were lent to her—were the same color as her dress and elevated her height to almost five-foot-six. She walked slowly, avoiding an embarrassing trip. She searched for the empty spot at the bar and approached the only vacant seat, right next to El Cadi.

"Hi! Is this seat taken?" she asked, lowering her tone and placing both her hands on the chair back.

El Cadi had been casually observing her. From his vantage point, he could see everyone who entered and exited the place, how many people were in the kitchen, how many waiters were and were not working on that shift, the number of locals and the number of tourists visiting the bar.

He, swizzling his drink, turned his head and peered over his shades to glance for a few seconds at the tight breasts that were telling him a story. He then looked up at the brown eyes covered in makeup. The black liner and the symmetry of her hair made her look like a descendant of Cleopatra.

"No," answered El Cadi, and he swallowed his drink.

"Great! It's so hot tonight!" she added in an almost two-tone melody.

"Hey, Papo! Give the lady whatever she wants!"

"Coming right up, *socio*," said the barman.

The barman approached the girl, placed a napkin with the Ron Don Q logo before her on the bar and extended his hands on the bar, waiting for her order.

"Uhm. I really don't know," she said giggling nervously. "I'll have what he's having," she said, pointing with her trembling hand to El Cadi's glass.

"Whiskey?" asked Papo.

"Whatever she wants," said El Cadi firmly, without taking his eyes off the girl's slim body. He placed a folded twenty on the bar's glossy scales.

She placed her clutch on the bar and pushed her hair behind her ears. Fascinated, she looked at the ophidian details of the alleged boa mounted on the sinuous piece of wood. Her dress was so tight, she had trouble accommodating her legs to sit. El Cadi place his mottled hand on her knee, and she was startled.

"Easy. Did you know *it's easier to find a good man in a bar than at church*?"

"Really?" she said, trying to hide her nervousness and brushing his hand away.

"Well, I read it in a novel, and I think it's true. Are you alone?"

"Yes."

"What's your name?"

"Camila," she lied. "What's yours?"

"Richard, but they call me El Cadi."

Papo placed the girl's drink on the napkin. She picked it up and, without stirring it she took a sip. She swallowed with difficulty and then gently coughed.

"It's a bit strong!" she said, putting her hand to her throat.

"You'll get used to it," said El Cadi. "If you like, I can soften it with some coconut water."

"Okay,' she said, moving her torso to the techno beat at the bar.

"Papo, some coconut water for the lady, please."

The barman immediately brought it over and moved away. El Cadi picked up the girl's glass and slowly added the coconut water. While stirring her drink, he dropped in a white powder concealed in his hand. She was too uncomfortable and distracted trying to sit on such a tall seat to notice. Still, she was satisfied she had found such an easy prey.

Piece of cake! All I have to do now is hit this zángano and get out of here before midnight. He'll be the first notch in my belt today. I'll win my way into Las Biz, she thought, feeling like the cunning and voluptuous *bad girl* in a cartoon series.

"Have you heard about the legend behind this bar?" asked El Cadi.

"I've heard something, but go on and tell me."

"Legend has it that it's simply a bar with an exotic boa scale design. But after midnight, when people have had too much to drink and lean against it, they see eyes, mouths, fingers and even tits made of silicone."

"No way!" she said. "I could use some."

"You? Not at all. Let me see," said El Cadi, extending his hand toward the girl's breasts.

"Uh, no, that's okay," she said, pushing his freckled hand away.

The two laughed mischievously.

El Cadi continued:

"Imagine, one evening, a client starting screaming after saying that he felt a snake tongue lick his mouth. He even felt the fiery venom going down his throat."

"Oh, come on!"

"I swear. He's never been back and the last I heard, he even quit drinking. Papo, another round here."

Chapter 9 – The Viper

El Cadi knew when the mixture of whiskey and the sleep-inducing powder would have the desired effect. He listened to the girl talk about the same old stories of failed relationships with boys, back-stabbing friends, and how clever she had been in getting back on her feet again. She was stretching the truth, of course. He sustained a slight smile while stirring his drink. He hadn't taken another sip. He nodded while listening and at times pushed, with his finger, the girl's hair behind her ear. She shivered at his touch. After swallowing the second drink with the powder, she let her guard down. She moved toward El Cadi and, in a sexy whisper in his ear, said: "Let's get out of here." He raised his eyebrows, stopped stirring his drink and looked at her. The bar's neon lights cast a sinister glow in his eyes.

El Cadi got up and pulled out his wallet. He knew that the girl's playing hard-to-get was part of the game; but if she were to back down, there should be no one around. When her eyelids and tongue were getting heavy, El Cadi suggested they go to his car. She thought that it was the perfect moment to carry out her plan, but she couldn't understand why, all of a sudden, she felt so heavy. He left another folded bill under the glass.

"Whoa, Cadi, this drink really had a kick to it!" she said, making an effort to keep her eyes open.

Suddenly, she noticed a vibration in her clutch.

"It's vibrating," she said, pointing to it and smiling mischievously.

She tried getting up, opening her clutch and pulling down her dress all at once, but all she could do was stumble onto El Cadi's chest. He held her arms. She realized that her dress had crept up to her upper thighs and her lower buttocks. Confused, she pulled it down forcefully on both sides. She stumbled; she was losing her bearings. The lights, the chairs and the tables were swirling liked a whirlwind around her. She even stifled a cry when she felt a strange touch coming from the bar. She closed her eyes and put her hand to her head.

I swear I felt a viper touching me, she thought in terror.

And El Cadi had thoughts of his own: *She's mine and I deserve a doll of flesh and bones. I'm tired of playing with Mother's dolls.*

El Cadi immediately grabbed her by the waist and carried the tripping girl to the parking lot. Her submissiveness only intensified his desire to touch her, drag her and throw her into the basement for torture. He wanted to see her on her knees, naked, willing to beg and do anything to be set free. He wanted to see that perfectly made-up face distorted with sweat and tears, with mascara staining her eyes and cheeks. He would become so aroused upon seeing, ever so closely, her chattering teeth under her swollen lips. He envisioned biting them until they were blue, almost about to burst. He was delirious with the thought of observing her eyes clamped open while he pulled out, one by one, her fake acrylic nails. Their designs reminded him of the coloring books he colored with chalk and tore to thousands of bits when he was a boy. In the end, he would cover her completely in white spray paint, a color that calmed El Cadi's nerves as it did his mother's.

With wings, El Cadi flew to the car. Nobody noticed anything, except for the owner of the bar whose eyes followed them to the exit. He knew who left with who each night, but he had not seen that girl before.

He thought, while digging his nose into checks and receipts, it must be her first time, but that's her problem.

"My purse! I can't leave...," she mumbled without ending her sentence.

Leaning on the side of the jeep, El Cadi looked left and right, like a hunter with fresh prey. The parking lot was full of empty cars. Nothing was stirring. Only an owl made accusatory sounds: *Who, who, youuu.* He was flattered by the owl.

El Cadi placed the girl in the passenger's seat and reclined it. She was stretched out. Standing by her side, he was aroused by her body, which seen from that angle was covered in moonlight. He had the desire to smell her. He drew closer to pick up the scent of her neck, her chest. She had the fragrance of his mother's doll, the first one he painted white when he was barely seven. He recalled his father's rage and his mother's screaming when she saw that her porcelain doll was ruined. El Cadi also recalled the pleasure in seeing his mother weeping, also smeared in white.

Bitch, he thought.

His father's punishment was still intact in his memory. Mr. Richard pushed him out from under the bed with a broomstick and threw him fully clothed in the shower under the cold water. And there, he beat him with his belt. The two cried. The father then grabbed him by the hair and locked him in an old closet. "Stay there until I tell you!" yelled the man. He remained in the closet until the following day when Mr. Richard unlocked the door. The boy was trembling from the cold and the fever. The father then tucked him in bed. The boy knew that the father was sorry, but his mother ignored him for a week. From that moment on, El Cadi loathed her, and he would take pleasure in seeing her die.

At the moment of his mother death, El Cadi licked his lips in satisfaction knowing that he was now the owner of her doll collection and that the dolls would be painted white, the way he wanted.

El Cadi looked left and right again. He turned to the girl. He pushed her thin shoulder dress straps down, exposing her braless breasts. He brutely kneaded her nipples. The girl whimpered, despite being almost unconscious.

It was then when a loud, young group walked out of the bar. El Cadi was startled and bumped his head against the car's roof. He swore and crouched to pick up his shades from the soiled asphalt, using his fingers like tweezers to gingerly pull them from the ground. He blew on his sunglasses and slid them into his shirt pocket. When he turned around, he saw the group scurrying away into the nearby brush behind the bar. They were going to smoke a few joints in the bar's rear terrace, where they could relax on the hammocks and rustic chairs. The rumor was that the buzz from the pot was more intense on that terrace because of its proximity to Puerto Diablo.

"Let's go, my little dolly," whispered El Cadi, leering at the intoxicated girl.

He went behind the car, got in and turned on the ignition. He turned to her again, ogling the mound between her legs.

You're still a girl. So young and such a little whore. Fuck it, I'm taking her with me. Ricky will be so happy, he thought.

El Cadi was sweating inside his car. He swept back the hair on his forehead and fixed his thick eyebrows. He placed his shades in their case. The car's tinted windows offered complete privacy. Wanting to leave quickly, he switched the gear to reverse, but then a hunger for sex struck him right then and there, and he switched the gear to neutral.

Like an eagle's talons, his hands bluntly spread apart the girl's thighs. His heart was now pounding, jumping, and he was panting. Sweat was running down his forehead and sideburns. His hand covered her left thigh completely. With her legs spread apart, her dress crept up to her groin. He drooled while pressing her desperately. Possessed by a wicked lewdness, he groped her and wanted more, but he held back.

No. It's better if I wait to do it in front of him, just to humiliate him. That way, he'll think I'm pleasing him. If he finds out I touched her, he might break my other doll. Poor Carmela, with her little white teddy bear, was completely broken, shattered. I'm still missing pieces of her face and hands. He's such an animal! But he still doesn't know who my favorite is. Yes, he does, because he's seen me talking to her. Shit. I'd better not provoke him. I'll use my saliva. Yes, only my tongue. It'll dry without a trace. Yes, only with saliva, thought El Cadi.

He grabbed her arm and started licking it. He then went to her face, her neck; he groped her breasts, and went down to her hips. Frantically, he squeezed her thighs and sunk his fingers into the folds of her sex. He muttered something and turned his head to the window. El Cadi observed her face and thought, *she won't wake up until noon tomorrow.*

A sound at the girl's feet jolted him. Again, the vibration inside her clutch. He hit the steering wheel with his fist. He knew he'd soon be breaking out in hives. In a fit of rage, he grabbed the purse, lowered the window and threw it out, downhill. He remained still and shut his eyes in rage.

I have to get out of here, he thought.

He grabbed his erect penis and pushed it down to hide it. Now, calmer, he closed his eyes while whiffing her odor on his fingers and he licked them. He pulled out a small pine tree shaped deodorizer from the glove compartment and rubbed it all over the girl. He shifted the gear into reverse and left the parking lot.

"When Ricky sees her, he'll see I'm better than him," repeated El Cadi on his way to La Hueca.

Chapter 10 - La Hueca

The strong westerly gusts shook the palm trees as El Cadi drove to La Hueca. The swaying fronds cast ghost-like shadows under the soft light of the moon. After a few miles on the main road in Barrio Esperanza, El Cadi saw a few drunken men struggling to walk straight on the sidewalks. Several yards ahead, on a terrace by the beach, he observed a group of young women—tourists—waiting for a bus to take them to some hotel to the northeast of Vieques. They took photos and selfies sticking out their tongues, with tall colorful glasses filled with drinks in their hands. El Cadi slowed down and fantasized about having an orgy with all of them. When he was done fantasizing, he continued on his way along Route 201 to La Hueca.

"We're home, my dolly," he whispered.

From the trunk he pulled out a small cache where he hid the remote control for the first electronic gate. He punched in the security code and continued on his way. Surrounding the home's perimeter was an electric fence. On the property, some thirty pine trees, all of the same height, offered additional protection. On both sides of the path leading to the garage, two large containers with white bougainvillea stood guard. In the middle of the property was a house painted in white. There was a balcony at the entrance with no seats or even a hammock beckoning rest. Jutting outside of the property was a huge steel mailbox with two locks.

It was timed so that when the first gate closed, the garage door opened. When everything was completely closed, the house was impenetrable. El Cadi made sure that no one entered the grounds. That way, he avoided all contact with anyone who might wander by. Once inside the garage, he looked into all the car mirrors and pushed the button to close the second electronic gate.

Before getting out of the car, El Cadi rested his head on the girl's chest and inhaled one more time. Possessed by a deep, corroding hatred he shook and slapped her hard. She was still out. He went from the garage to the kitchen and in anger threw his soiled shades in the garbage. He then pulled out a beer from the refrigerator. He carefully looked at the kitchen. Everything was in its place. He gulped down his beer in two sips, rinsed out the can, threw it in the aluminum recycling bin and washed his hands with plenty of soap. He was ready to see Ricky.

He looked up at the kitchen's white ceiling and breathed in and out with short pauses in between. He walked toward the house's two bedrooms. In one of them, was a passage to the basement. In the first room, with the air conditioning at a constant 69 degrees, there was a gigantic television screen with a surround-sound system throughout the whole room, and several boxes containing video games, remote controls, and earplugs. In the middle of the room, on a shaggy white rug, there were two bone-white leather reclining massage chairs. The connected antenna system was programmed to turn the television on at certain hours to the CV-SEX channel. The shelves against one of the walls displayed different collections featuring porn stars: Candy, Susie, Lolita, Toby, Superman, The Child Project, as well as all the versions of Caligula. A corner on the top shelf had a collection of some TV crime series: *Dexter, CSI* and *Bones*. In the other bedroom there was a queen-sized bed covered in a white satin quilt that once belonged to his parents. The room had only one window, and below it was a simple dresser with nine drawers. There were two doors on opposite sides of the room. The one on the left led to the bathroom, and the one on the right was locked. From one of the dresser drawers he pulled out a key and unlocked the door leading to the basement. He grabbed the pillar candle he always kept lit on the small altar with a photo of his mother scribbled in white chalk. From that ghostly image sprang the woman's dark eyes. El Cadi walked down several steep steps, holding on to the wall with his free hand. Ricky was waiting for him.

"Fleeing?" asked the calm man's voice from the bottom of the basement.

El Cadi stopped for a second to determine from where exactly the voice came. *He must be lying in bed, watching one of his movies or films*, he thought. He then took five more steps and heard him get up from the futon.

"No, I'm not fleeing. Open the curtain," ordered El Cadi while flicking the switch on the wall that lit the blue-hued area.

A large, mottled hand slowly slid the silk curtain. Behind it was a man.

"Cadi, sister dear, you have to turn the temperature down a bit. I got hives again today. I look like an albino worm in this damned hole. What's this jungle called, Bieke?"

"Vieques, Ricky. And if you call me *sister dear* again, I'll crank the temperature up just to see you squirm. Plus…"

"Just joking, *Cadicito*. I only called you that because you remind me of Dolly, that demented woman. Remember when you put on her night gown?" He paused. "Besides, so what?"

"Dumbass! Dolly may have been crazy, but she was also your mother, and she didn't punish *you*. In fact, you were her favorite. Actually no, she was afraid of you."

"Are you stupid, Cadi? She was never a mother to us. Have you forgotten that already?"

"Let's leave it alone. Look at yourself now! Just forget it and listen," said El Cadi, keeping a safe distance from the metal bars separating them.

"There must be good news if you're waking me at this hour," answered Ricky, tensing all the muscles in his face and arms.

"Yes, there is, in the form of a doll; a real doll made of flesh and bones. My first real woman."

"Ah, that's my little brother, always looking out for me and pleasing me."

Ricky was El Cadi's identical twin. Shaking his head twice to one side and, closing his eyes, he licked his lips. With the tips of his fingers, he gently caressed the cell's bars, as if painting them with delicate brushstrokes.

Chapter 11 – The Richards

Mr. Richard, the twins' father, had been keeping Ricky in a cell since 1998. After the horrid death of his wife Dolly, he went into hiding with his two boys in the outlying Canadian city of Winnipeg. The widower was now planning the details of a new beginning.

His boys' twisted lives kept alive memories of a dark past that started with his marriage to Dolly.

They told me arranged marriages were full of surprises, he recalled when, months after exchanging their vows, he heard his wife babbling nonsense to her doll collection. *I guess it's because she's an only child,* he thought. On some nights he was awakened by her screams and would find her banging her head against the wall. And then she would point to him and laugh hysterically for no apparent reason. *Am I that ugly? Is it me?* he wondered, again convinced of his bad luck with women. He married a wacko this time.

Dolly's schizophrenia worsened during her pregnancy.

A child with this woman... he thought, as she excitedly showed him the results of her pregnancy test.

"It'll be a baby girl. No, a princess. She'll wear dresses and ribbons and satin shoes. I'll comb her hair and she'll wear headbands in all colors. Oh, and her room; how will I decorate her room? Her toys...." She went on and on.

Meanwhile, Mr. Richard, with helpless resignation would think: *Will the baby inherit her craziness? Good God!*

Dolly's grandparents immigrated from Germany and settled in the Midwestern United States, bringing with them their porcelain doll business. Even before Dolly was born, she inherited hundreds of porcelain dolls all carefully preserved by her mother and grandmother.

As her mother and grandmother did before her, Dolly talked about wanting a baby girl to dress like her dolls. Her world was her Little Kingdom, consisting of rooms with flowers and stuffed toys and unicorns and tea sets. Everything was for her dolls. As a child, she had little tolerance for interruptions. If something unexpected pulled her out of her imaginary conversations, she would immediately throw a tantrum, screaming and crying until her parents could take it no longer. That was how she was raised.

When Dolly was a young woman, her father called her into his office to say that she would be marrying in three months' time. He then handed her the title deed to a property as a wedding gift. Her father was shocked when she held out her hand, snatched the paper from him and said: "At last, my dolls will have a room of their own. It will be called The Little Kingdom. Thanks, Daddy."

Mr. Richard and Dolly lived near her family. He managed his own car-rental business. He worked nearly twelve hours a day, but after finding out they were going to have twins, he became more considerate and hired a nanny.

Dolly, meanwhile, could think of nothing other than the birth of her princesses. She spent the days shopping for baby clothes and matching accessories. Sometimes when her husband got home from work, she was already asleep. Their relationship was basically non-existent.

When she went into labor on Nov. 1, 1984, the nurses at the Midland Medical Center, in Michigan, could not understand why Dolly would not stop crying. Her two babies had been born. She went so far as to hold the nurses responsible for a security breach in the hospital and insisted that her husband had swapped her twin girls for two squawking redheaded boys. A hospital official went along with her and feigned taking down information for the complaint. As accustomed as the official was to a new mother's fluctuating hormones, this was the first time someone had complained about something like this.

Dolly was even more convinced of the switch. When Mr. Richard ordered that the two boys to be named after him: Richard II and Richard III, she hated him, she hated the three. Her maternal instinct never saw the light of day. She cried in the hospital, at home, at church, in the doctor's office, at the market..., she cried until her weeping turned into incessant conversations with her dolls. Only her dolls made her happy. She did not want those two little phonies near her.

Dolly's family told Mr. Richard to hire a nanny, the way they had done when she was born.

"It's better for everyone," said the parents of the new mother. So he did.

Immersed in his work, Mr. Richard had no part in rearing the boys. He left the house and returned when they were asleep. Each night after supper, he sat and listened for hours to Dolly's chatter about The Little Kingdom. If, by chance, he asked something about the twins, she acted as if she did not know what he was talking about.

The twins grew up in rooms decorated with rainbows, clouds, trees with flowers, birds and sunrays all painted by an artist hired by their grandmother. The curtains matched the sheets, the walls, the chair cushions.

The boys had another room with an endless collection of toys: miniature houses, books, classic Disney movies with princesses, balls, dinosaurs, board games and even an inflatable clown named McDonald.

Dolly kept The Little Kingdom room locked, believing that the twins might ruin her collection of over a hundred porcelain dolls, most of them made in Germany and France. Each doll had a name. She even commissioned a glass box. Inside the box was a small, red velvet cushion with gold tassels, on which she placed a record she called the Sacred Codex. In it, she recorded and traced the history and lineage of each doll. Some of the dolls even had their own legends, poems, songs, and stories written by her or by previous owners. Once the twins learned to walk, they were forbidden from entering that room.

Already in the third grade, the boys were home from school one afternoon and Ricky turned the door handle to that forbidden room. The door opened. He looked to the left and to the right and pushed the door further. It squeaked slightly, but now wide open, it offered him a whole new space.

His mother was baking a birthday cake for one of her dolls, because the nanny called in sick that day. Ricky signaled to his brother, and Cadi immediately appeared. As usual, they did not need to talk in order to understand each other. The two were entering the secret room for the very first time and were fascinated by all the dolls. They looked like small, living beings, so a frightened Cadi remained at the door. There were hundreds of porcelain faces under curly, straight or wavy hair. Some of the dolls were standing; others were seated on chairs proportionately fitted for them. A good many had purses matching their dresses; others had toys, stuffed animals and even toy pets at their feet: dogs, cats, turtles, birds. In the center was a pale-yellow table painted with rose and violet flower buds. From each flower sprang green vines that crept down the table legs and disappeared into the white rug. On the table, under venetian lace doilies, were four teacups with their saucers waiting for teatime. In the middle were the tea kettle and the sugar holder on a silver tray.

Ricky grabbed a black-haired doll with blue eyes, in an unusual green shamrock printed dress. A small tag at her feet identified her as *Susan, The Black Irish*. Ricky thought it would be the perfect gift for his eighth birthday. He lifted the doll's skirt. From the door, terrified without uttering a word, Cadi observed his brother. The two were startled when suddenly they heard their mother's voice coming from the kitchen.

"Let's go!" whispered Cadi.

Ricky grabbed the doll by the hair, stuffed her in his school shirt and looked at his brother. Cadi nodded and headed toward the kitchen. Ricky went to the room the two shared and whistled twice. Dolly was talking on the phone while decorating the cake in yellow frosting. Cadi did not want to interrupt her. He saw she was busy, turned around and headed to his room. Ricky had already undressed the doll and covered her with a white mixture of liquid glue from head to toe. The doll was on the bed, but she would not close her eyes, so Ricky found tape to cover her eyes and keep the doll from staring at him. Cadi got closer, but his brother held out his arm. Ricky moved the doll to his desk and started to brush the glue on her feet, and licked his fingers when he guided the brush up between the doll's legs. He continued up the torso, then the face and the black curls, which turned stiff and lost their luster under the glue. The child blew on her several times to dry her. He then laid her down with her back facing up.

"Now it's your turn," he ordered Cadi, handing him the brush dripping with glue.

Cadi approached cautiously and managed to avoid getting glue on his fingers. There was a grimace of disgust on his face. As always, he followed his brother's orders, unable to understand why he wielded such power over him. While he was brushing the doll's hair with glue, the mother entered the room.

"Mother!" yelled Ricky.

Dolly dropped the cake she was holding when she saw her doll on the boys' desk. She was on the verge of fainting. She opened and closed her eyes several times. Cadi dropped the brush on the doll and wiped his hands on his pants. Ricky pointed to his brother and kept his eyes on his mother at all times.

"Cadi, what have you done?" she said gritting her teeth while closing in on him.

She kept her eyes on him while snatching the stiff, white doll from the desk.

"Neither of you will leave here until tomorrow," she screamed unhinged, pressing the doll against her chest. "And you," she said pointing to Cadi, "You'll see when your father comes home. I hope he kills you," she hissed, and she shut the door.

Dolly remained in the hallway unable to move. She shut her eyes and inhaled enough air to let out a steady, shrill stream of condemnations, railing *how bad they were, how she never loved them, how they were a mistake and not her real children.*

With one hand she clutched her doll, with the other she pulled her own hair, sweat rolling down the nape of her neck, her forehead, and the sides of her face. She then remembered that the cake was now in bits and pieces scattered between the twins' room and the hallway, and let out another even longer wail. She sobbed in distress, as if she were a child again. She sucked her right ring finger, held the doll tenderly to her chest and went to her room.

The boys looked at each other. For Cadi, everything went blank. His body shook and he felt feverish. He wiped his eyes with his shirt and saw such a calm expression on Ricky that it sent chills down his spine. Cadi was sweating. The twins did not point fingers at each other or even exchange words. Ricky glanced at his desk and sat down to do his homework. And Cadi, who had pissed his pants, stood there waiting for the inevitable.

All was silent in the house. They only sound came from the bathtub faucet opening and closing over and over. At times, the water pulsed through the pipes and resonated through the metal. And Dolly could be faintly heard singing a lullaby.

That evening, however, the twins were paralyzed with fear when they heard the garage door open at precisely seven o'clock. Dolly was seated in the informal dining room with the doll wrapped in a white towel. Through the door, the boys could hear the soliloquy of accusations accompanied by sobbing and yelling. The twins waited in their room. At that moment, they actually believed the death threat Dolly wished upon them.

Mr. Richard listened until she started to repeat the story. He then lifted a hand as a sign for her to stop. He went to the hallway closet, pulled out the broom and walked to the twins' room. Ricky pointed to under the bed, where the suspect was hiding. The father, wasting no time, started thrashing under the bed with the broom. Cadi crawled out bawling all the pent-up anguish accrued since three that afternoon. No questions were asked. Mr. Richard grabbed him by the ear, pulled him to the bathroom opened the shower and drenched him. He then pushed him into a closet and left him there until the next day. Cadi was punished for the two. And he would never forget it.

Despite the punishment, the twins' desire to visit the dolls' room again increased with each passing day. There were nights when the two brothers laid awake talking about every detail of their first visit to the room.

Ricky wanted the dolls, but Cadi would be content merely observing in detail how perfect each one was. Mother made it difficult for them to carry out their plans by placing double locks on the door this time.

Four years passed. At twelve, the twins were robust, like little wrestlers. One afternoon, during carpentry class in their junior-high school, Ricky whistled to his brother. Near them was the teacher's bag of tools. Cadi grabbed the ones his brother pointed to and hid them in his backpack.

The twins, joined by their mother's contempt and their father's indifference, would carry out their plan. Nobody looked after them now that they were grown. One day, when their mother was away from the house, they took apart the locks guarding The Little Kingdom. Once again, they entered the forbidden. This time Ricky grabbed two of the tallest dolls. Cadi fell in love with the one that had a stuffed toy bear. He caressed its smooth hair and put it back. He then was drawn to another doll the same height as the one his brother had. They left the broken locks on the floor and went to their room.

The ceremony lasted several hours. With pent-up anger, they undressed the dolls and examined their rigid bodies. With no sense of shame at all, they groped the areas their nanny called the genitals. Ricky drew pubic hair and nipples on them with a fine-point marker. On the other side of the bed, Cadi combed their hair; but then he would feel his brother's gaze and he would tousle their hair and open their legs in a split, as if the dolls were gymnasts. They searched every hole they could find on the dolls, even ones behind their ears, and they closely examined the tiny tufts of fake hair on their heads. Then Ricky came up with an idea and ordered his brother to pull down his pants and fondle his penis. Ricky laughed at his brother's clumsiness.

"Cadi, you're such an asshole! That's not how you do it. Watch me," he said, showing him how to masturbate.

Ricky's feverish action ended in a moan of pleasure. They both rubbed their viscid fluids on the naked dolls. Ricky laughed manically at how he, in utter pleasure, was destroying that which their mother loved most. Cadi followed him. Tired of jerking off, they looked for the glue Ricky kept in his desk. Cadi placed the dolls, one next to the other, on the bed. Ricky covered their eyes with tape and proceeded to mummify the fronts of their bodies with toilet paper and glue. Cadi mummified their backs. Before they were even dry, the twins carried the dolls to Dolly's room and placed them on her bed. Dolly would be home soon.

El Cadi grabbed his mother's only bottle of perfume. The twins filled the bathtub with water and emptied the bottle in it. They masturbated again, spewing their fluids into the aromatic water as they laughed. El Cadi undressed and donned his mother's bathrobe and high heels while softly singing a made-up song. Ricky went to his room, pulled out the hammer from his backpack and, with astonishing determination, hid it behind a vase in the bathroom. They heard their mother's soft footsteps in the kitchen. She left her bag on the table and headed to the hallway. She screamed in horror upon seeing the locks to the dolls' room on the floor. She ran to her room. The door was also open, although she usually left it ajar before going out. She slowed her pace and, before even crossing the threshold, she saw the three porcelain dolls covered in white and she tilted her head to the right. El Cadi, dressed up like a doll, was there beside them; he looked at her. Dolly opened her mouth to scream, but before she could emit a sound, Ricky—who was by the bathroom door—sarcastically said, "Mother, we've prepared a special bath for you."

El Cadi was closer, so she went for him, ready to strangle him.

"I told you to stay away from my dolls!" she yelled, without letting go of his neck.

Possessed by some superhuman force, she shook El Cadi like a rag doll.

"Let him go!" ordered Ricky.

The woman did not stop. El Cadi's eyes were about to burst, and his lips were turning blue as he tried, in vain, to grab her face.

Ricky, meanwhile, was enjoying every minute of it, but he was then angered over the fact that his plans had now shifted. From the room's closet, he tore off a plastic bag covering one of Dolly's dresses and, pouncing on his mother, slipped the bag over her head and neck. The three fell to the floor, and Ricky wacked Dolly's head until she was unconscious. She lay motionless while El Cadi, now freed from her grip, gasped for air.

"You're useless. You were supposed to hit her with the hammer," yelled Ricky. "Get up and help me."

Ricky searched for Dolly's pulse. She was still alive. He removed her clothes but left the bag over her head and neck. El Cadi got up shakily and helped his brother carry her. One grabbed her by the arms, while the other grabbed her by the legs. The two carried her to the bathroom and placed her in the Roman style tub. As her body sank, the two took pleasure in seeing the bubbles floating out of her nose and mouth. All of a sudden, as if Dolly's body had grown tentacles, she tried with all her might to get out of the water.

"Get on her legs!" ordered Ricky.

El Cadi sat on his mother's thighs, while his brother pushed her head in the water, stifling a cry of pent-up rage.

They remained on her in silence for twenty minutes. Their faces were wet, even though neither shed as much as a tear in remorse. The two then broke into laughter that grew so wildly, it reverberated on the naked walls of the bathroom.

"What will we do now?" asked El Cadi trembling when his brother stopped laughing.

"Don't be such an idiot! It was an accident. I'll talk to Father. Understood? Help me clean up here so he doesn't find us wet."

Chapter 12 - White Dolly

El Cadi was upset over what happened with Dolly. He trembled. He took a bath, just as Ricky ordered, and washed his hands every ten minutes even though they were clean. He exuded sweat as if it were shame. He changed clothes twice.

They'll blame me again. I know they will. Was it my fault? Maybe if I hadn't worn her robe, she might still be alive. Oh, Dolly, my Mother...Mother? Never! But her shoes looked so nice on me. Oh no, she's dead! Is she dead? Maybe she held her breath and...No! She's dead! She's under water. This is terrible! I can still see her eyes! Should I look at her one last time? No. Ricky doesn't want me to go back. I could leave behind clues. Ricky killed her. He did it! I didn't do anything!

The twins' mother had been dead for two hours. Ricky took charge, giving El Cadi orders, and pulling off the bag from Dolly's head. The killer and his accomplice looked at her face one last time. Ricky smiled. El Cadi covered his mouth in fear and ran to the toilet to vomit.

Wuss, thought Ricky. He licked his right middle finger, placed it on Dolly's forehead and again pushed her into the water. He was cocky, now looking down on her the way she often looked at him. He stifled the desire to spit on her. He then dried the floor with a white towel, changed the bathroom rugs, placed the plastic bag in his backpack along with the tools he took from school, and returned the dolls embalmed in glue back to where they belonged: to Dolly's fantasy kingdom. Very calmly, he set up the locks and locked the door to the dolls' room, and he placed all the wet items, including their clothes, in a bag he deposited in their neighbor's garbage can.

Before entering the house again through the garage, he looked up at sky, opened his arms, and sighed. He was pleased. Once inside, he closed the garage door and summoned his brother.

Without uttering a word, the twins met in the formal dining room. Ricky sat at one end on top of the rectangular table. El Cadi sat on a chair at the opposite end. Dolly never allowed them to sit on those chairs upholstered in fine Portuguese fabric. They glanced at each other in silence. There, they waited two hours for their father to arrive. As they waited, Ricky casually leafed through the women's lingerie section in the Sears catalog. He would skip to the toy section and then would go back many times to look at the women clad only in undergarments, albeit made up and coifed for a cocktail party. El Cadi remained silent. He looked at his hands and would wipe the sweat on his face with his sleeve. He fidgeted, moving his hands to the front, to the back, and then he would cross his arms. At times, he would put his hands together and again interlace his fingers. When he felt his brother's gaze, he would hide his hands under his thighs, only to free them shortly after and start over. He took deep breaths and exhaled in short pauses.

At seven on the dot Mr. Richard got home. Ricky quickly got off the table and sat straight up in the chair. As always, the father entered through the kitchen and dropped his key in the key basket. He found it odd not to smell food or see Dolly seated at the minibar between the breakfast nook and the stove. She always welcomed him there with a beer to talk about her dolls before serving him dinner. He looked for her in the informal dining room and to his surprise, he found the twins seated on the elegant chairs.

"What are you doing there? Where's your mother? Is there no dinner today?"

Ricky and El Cadi looked at each other.

"We wanted to tell you something. Maybe you should sit down?" answered Ricky slowly. El Cadi glanced at the floor and hid his hands again.

"Well, what happened now?"

Mr. Richard approached the head of the table to take a good look at his sons. As he sat down, he hoped to hear about some funny event of the day that Dolly would not have found amusing at all.

"It's Dolly; she's dead," said Ricky almost with an aristocratic air, sitting straight, with his head high, his face showing no emotion. The boy held his father's gaze without so much as blinking.

"What?"

"She apparently slipped in the tub. Since she didn't answer, we opened the door. Cadi and I found her there in the water."

Mr. Richard's eyes and mouth grew wide. The word *dead* ricocheted through his head like a gunshot. His cunning smile contorted into a grimace, making his face look like the Greek Tragedy Mask. Before Ricky finished speaking, Mr. Richard clumsily got up, overturning the chair in the process. He ran to the bedroom and confirmed his son's words: Dolly was submerged in the bathtub. Her stiff, naked body was covered in hundreds of tiny, transparent hives. Her hair still seemed to have some life to it though, swaying like algae in the water.

Mr. Richard put one foot in the tub and pulled her out by her armpits. He placed the rigid corpse on the edge of the tub. He then grabbed a nearby white towel, folded it three times and placed it under her neck. The trembling man lifted his eyebrows and shook his head. He was horrified. He sensed the lie in the air. He sighed, in dismay.

I was always so absent, he thought.

Left with no answers, he lowered his head, but lifted it again as if coming up with a grand idea to solve it all. In a final goodbye, he kissed Dolly's forehead.

"Poor woman. I knew. I knew it," he whispered, gently pushing aside her hair, observing the petrified look on her face.

"What do you know?" asked Ricky from the bathroom door.

"Nothing, son. Go to your room."

"Why?"

"Enough, already!" he yelled. "Go to your room now!"

Ricky obeyed. Mr. Richard left the body on the edge of the bathtub. On his way to the kitchen, he closed the door to Ricky's room. He then called the police.

El Cadi was still seated in the dining room, waiting for orders from either Ricky or his father. Mr. Richard approached him, picked up the chair and turned it to confront him. Their faces were a mere two inches apart, and they breathe, so closely that the carbon dioxide of one became the oxygen of the other.

"Look at me. What happened? Tell me the truth."

El Cadi lifted his head. His father's distorted face, seeming as if it had aged years, terrified him. El Cadi had never seen him like that, or perhaps he had not seen him this close.

"And Ricky?" asked El Cadi as sweat ran down his face and neck, drenching his clothes even more.

"He's in his room. Don't worry. Tell me everything before the police get here."

For the first time, El Cadi felt freed from the twisted umbilical cord binding him to his brother. As he confessed to his father, he realized then and there—without actually intending to—that he now had control over his brother. He molded the story to best suit him, and overemphasized Ricky's role in it. He told his father of his brother's unruly behavior: of how he stole the tools; of how he forced him, controlled him, and coerced him under threat to participate in his scheme. With a shaky voice, he ended his confession by saying that Ricky threatened to kill him as well if he did not take part in the plot to kill Dolly. He depicted his brother as a young, cold executioner, and described the cruelty with which he drowned his mother. His own truth freed him from his identical twin's captivity and in silence, he became the self-proclaimed heir of the doll collection.

Mr. Richard lowered his head and scratched his forehead. He interrupted Cadi and ordered him to follow him to Ricky's room.

"Look," said the father firmly as he rolled his wet sleeves. "The police are on their way and will interrogate us. Cadi, remember what Ricky said, that you called your mother, but she didn't respond? And then you went to the bathroom and found her in the tub?" he said, adding an exasperated, "Well dammit! At least show some grief now! Go to the bathroom, put soap in your eyes and shed a fucking tear at least! You devils!"

From afar, they could hear the wailing ambulance. The police car followed. Two officers and several emergency workers parked their vehicles in front of the house. A few neighbors peered through their windows, but no one ventured out. The cold weather, it seemed, heightened neighborhood apathy, freezing any sign of human kindness and even curiosity.

One of the officers knocked on the door three times, each knock bringing the Grim Reaper's reach closer. Mr.

Richard opened the door and led them to the bathroom. As the paramedics felt Dolly's neck for signs of life, one of the investigators observed all details, searching for clues. Everything was clean, immaculate, except for the puddles of water next to the tub and hundreds of wet footprints in different directions throughout the house. There were no traces of blood on the floor or the walls. Everything was in its place. Everything was white.

I wish my wife had the house as nice as this, thought the detective while snapping photographs he considered worthy of an interior decorating magazine.

The other officer took the widower aside first for interrogation. Mr. Richard, seated on the edge of the sofa in the formal living room, smoothed his hair back with both hands and heaved a deep sigh. He then repeated what Ricky had told him, stressing that he was not home when the *accident* occurred. The officer scribbled the man's words in a yellowish notebook splattered with grease, its edges worn.

It was then Ricky's turn. He obeyed his father, and started whining, almost unintelligibly emitting a few phrases: "Mom, mommy drowned. I called her and she didn't answer."

Finally, came Cadi. With his hands together, his legs crossed and without making eye contact with the officer, he said he did not want to see his mother because he was afraid. His eyes cried and his nose ran until he fell asleep in the chair's wide arms. Mr. Richard woke him and accompanied him to bed.

The detective told the paramedics they could leave. When the youngest one was gathering his equipment, he asked the detective: "Drowned?"

The officer, punching a number into his cell phone, paused and curtly retorted: "What do you think?"

"I don't know. You're the expert."

"No, actually I'm not. I'm dialing the coroner's office. Good evening," he said with indifference, and headed into the hallway.

Midnight was already approaching. Mr. Richard, seated in the living room with the two police officers, was waiting on the medical investigators and the coroner to arrive for the removal of the body. The long wait was irking him, and he had no time to waste. He had a plan to carry out. He observed, without blinking, the only photo of his sons on one of the living room walls. They were only little boys. The police officers kept an eye on him as they exchanged among themselves their impressions on sports and the latest news.

They were interrupted by a cell phone ringing.

"Officer Miller speaking," answered the policeman, and after a long pause, he added, "A fatal accident at M-20. That many? Huh, I see. Geez! Okay, I'll tell them. Thanks for the information. Bye."

"What happened?" asked his partner.

"There was an accident on the highway to Michigan and the two coroners on this shift are there with their personnel. Several fatalities." He looked at Mr. Richard and continued, "They won't be here until the early morning."

"Wow! Until then...!" said the other officer in a discouraging grin.

"Luckily, we only have a P.A.D. here," said Agent Miller, code for *Possible Accidental Death.*

His partner put his finger to his lips, signaling him to keep quiet. He kept him from babbling on by saying: "I'm going out to grab a bite. What do you want?"

"Where are you going?"

"McDonald's. There's always one close by."

"I want a number one combo meal with a large coffee," said Miller, pulling out his wallet from his pants pocket.

"Would you like something to eat?" he asked Mr. Richard.

"No, thank you."

When the officer left, Mr. Richard asked Miller what was going to happen to his wife.

"I'm very sorry but your wife's body has to stay where it is until the coroner and his crew arrive and order its removal. They'll take the body to the forensics center in the city of Saline and leave it there until it's time for the examination and autopsy. With the pending cases and with the accident, I'm guessing your wife's body will be ready in two or three days."

Mr. Richard clenched his jaw and hung his head. The officer put away his cell phone and pulled out a roll of yellow tape with black letters from his bag. He apologized to the widower and headed to the last bedroom, where Dolly laid.

It looks like Dolly will remain in the water, naked, with not even a wake. That's so cruel, thought the widower.

Officer Miller marked an X on the door to the couple's bedroom with the yellow tape. It was now off limits until the coroner arrived. The sight of Ricky's figure in the hallway startled the officer. The teenager stared at him, as if he were in a trance. The policeman called the father who rushed over and, apologizing, he grabbed his son by the shoulders and directed him to his room. Ricky casually glanced at the scene. Everything was under control, the way he wanted.

The father tucked him in and caressed his hair. Ricky pushed his hand away, turned toward the window and imagined his new world without Dolly. He closed his eyes and smiled in satisfaction.

There was a slight knock on the front door. Mr. Richard, on his way out of the hall, opened it. It was the other officer carrying a few pungent bags of hamburgers and fries. In his other hand, he had a cardboard box with two large cups and two smaller ones.

"The coffees were free," said the officer with a contented grin. Mr. Richard allowed them to sit at the formal dining table. As the officers settled in, he brought them a garbage bag and asked them to please deposit any garbage or remains in the bag and to take it outside.

Upon seeing the officers' looks of surprise, he added: "I'm sorry, officers, but my wife would have wanted it that way. If you wish, you can leave it all on the table and tomorrow I'll…"

"Say no more. We'll do as you wish."

"It doesn't matter. I think I'm going to rest for a while. I'll be in the first room on the right."

"Good night," said the policemen.

Mr. Richard settled in the guest room and bolted his door shut. He feared for his life, and yet he felt responsible for his boys. He could not sleep. He was overwhelmed by an uncertain future. He was aware of how the mother had damaged the twins beyond repair. He envisioned taking them away from the nest where they were malformed. And that was what he would do. They would move to a tropical paradise where the sun could provide the boys with a new environment, where they would be surrounded by warm, friendly people.

So much cold and loneliness can drive you mad, he thought.

He wanted a new life for them, regardless of whether it was in another country with a different culture and language. He wanted a new environment to do away with their old identities. He would struggle to make sure the memory of their mother remained hidden in a small corner of their minds. He would keep tabs on his sons' mental health. They would be reborn.

The sun rose, and the coroner and several forensic technicians finally arrived at the home. The coroner, his shirt rumpled and his hair disheveled, was carrying a doctor's bag and in the other hand he held a cup of coffee emblazoned with his name.

One of the technicians knocked and Officer Miller opened the door. After a brief greeting, they went over to the bedroom, now crucified with yellow tape that repeatedly read: *Crime Scene Do Not Cross.*

The policemen whispered their findings to the newcomers. The coroner visited the four corners of the bathroom and carefully examined the walls, the floor, the collection of jars containing beauty and bath products, the mirror, until finally going over to the body. He pulled out a pair of blue, disposable gloves and put them on. He tenderly touched and examined Dolly's head, her temples, the sides of her face, the top of her head, the back of her head, and her neck. He then examined her face and ordered one of his crew to take close-up pictures of her eyes, her nose and mouth.

"Hmmm!" was the only thing the coroner said.

He pulled off his gloves, threw them on the floor and whistled the way one calls a dog. The technicians sprung to work, removing the body from the water. They placed it on its side to keep the stiff curvature of its back from getting in the way of the body bag's zipper. As they were wheeling the body up the hall, Mr. Richard came out of the guest room all disheveled, wearing the same clothes as the previous day.

"Expect a call from us," said one of the investigators.

After Dolly's body was removed, the widower made several calls. He withdrew all his money from the bank and sold all his shares. He rented a van and, in the afternoon, the three set out to Canada. It would take them two or three days to get there. In the black market, Mr. Richard was able to get a new identity for himself and the twins, and he opened a bank account under his new surname. To keep from further traumatizing, the boys, the three kept their first names: Richard, Richard II (Ricky), and Richard III (Cadi).

He asked several Salvadorian men—who for years had been waiting to obtain American citizenship—to move their belongings that same evening. They would move only what was on the list: two bedroom sets, the dining and living room furniture, their clothes, plus the doll collection—a special request from Cadi.

"Remember what happened yesterday?" asked Mr. Richard privately to Cadi.

"Yes," answered the boy, and he immediately started scratching his arms.

"You have to keep it a secret to protect Ricky. To protect us all."

"But Daddy, we're in danger," whispered Cadi.

"Yes, I know. He's your brother and he's sick. I have a plan and I'm counting on you to help him. Do you understand?"

El Cadi looked left, right and back, making sure Ricky was not hiding, listening to their conversation.

"What's wrong, son?"

"Can I have something special from Mama?"

"What?"

"Her dolls. I want them all."

"But…," said a puzzled Mr. Richard.

"I want the dolls! I want the dolls" yelled Cadi several times.

"Shh! Okay, we'll take the dolls with us, but only if you keep our secret," said Mr. Richard, strongly holding his son by the shoulders.

Their belongings would remain stashed away in a clandestine warehouse until further notice.

Chapter 13 - Vieques, The Paradise

It cost Mr. Richard a lot of money, but in less than six months he was able to radically change his life and the lives of the twins. Through the internet he found out that he and his boys were on the wanted list in the United States. They were not on the most dangerous list, but were wanted, nonetheless. The man cut all contact with family and friends in Michigan. Dolly's elderly parents, horrified over the news of her death, were terribly worried over their son-in-law's and grandsons' disappearance.

The investigation into Dolly's death yielded no further clues. Even though the case was not a high priority, it remained open, still.

Mr. Richard and his boys hid in Canada for several months. In January of 1998, the father took a risk and traveled alone to an island in the Caribbean, where he would have no trouble showing his Canadian passport.

The tropics will be a good change of venue for my boys, he thought.

The stunning island of Vieques would serve as their den for hiding their old, inner demons. Mr. Richard's plans included setting up a car rental business for tourists there. He contacted one of the local dwellers with *friends in the government* to help him rush through the required permit and licensing process. Without any announcement, he set up the car rental business near the port of Isabel II, catching people off guard as a competitor with others in the same line of business.

He hired several undocumented workers from the western area of Puerto Rico and took them to Vieques—with all expenses paid—to work on his property. They had to remodel a home in Barrio La Hueca to include certain specifications not suited for life on a tropical island. For one, they had to build a cell in the basement. Once the home was remodeled, Mr. Richard went to fetch Cadi.

"Everything's ready. It'll be easy; you'll see," he said to his son. Throughout those first days, the father could be seen about Vieques with only one son. The other one would be invisible to the residents.

The house was painted white both inside and out. It was sparsely furnished and had nothing appealing that could draw attention. In a month, their belongings would arrive, including that which was most important to Cadi: the doll collection. Mr. Richard left the boy in the house with enough provisions, clean clothes, and a collection of videogames and movies to last a week, until he came back from Canada with Ricky.

It was noon, and the heat was beating down on the people of Isla Nena. Ricky arrived with his father at the Rivera Rodríguez Airport. It was Mr. Richard's third trip to Vieques, and Ricky's first. Some of the residents though they had seen those same faces the week before. Father and son were so alike; besides, not many redheads lived on that island of approximately nine thousand people.

From the airport they took a taxi. Ricky's eyes followed the girls in worn out clothes, running barefoot. He lowered the taxi's window, leaned his head back and closed his eyes. In the darkness he felt the salty breeze tousling his hair. He was tired after the long trip from Canada. Without warning, the car hit the brakes and then started riding in reverse.

"We're here," said Mr. Richard.

The taxi driver helped him unload the suitcases and offered to take them inside, but his offer was declined.

Inside, El Cadi was watching a crime series and eating popcorn. When he heard them arrive, he got up from the chair to pick up several empty soda cans he threw about here and there. He looked at his father and then Ricky. There were no hellos, no hugs, no kisses.

"Leave your suitcase here," he ordered Ricky. And with the old trick of *I'm going to show you something I know you'll love*, Mr. Richard and El Cadi led Ricky to the basement. Without much effort, they locked him in a small cell with air conditioning and a small TV set. This was his new room.

"You think I'm surprised? I'm hungry," was the only thing Ricky said. Mr. Richard and El Cadi looked at him in silence. They then went upstairs to finish settling in.

Chapter 14 - Witnesses to History

It was August of 2012. The Richards had been in Vieques for fourteen years. El Cadi was enthralled by the charm of the most wondrous island in the Caribbean. That was what he thought as he enjoyed his adolescence and young adulthood on an island guarded by topaz blue seas that had everything: an airport, a wharf, hotels, churches, town squares, a theater, bars, museums, lagoons, a bio-luminescent bay, hundreds of wild horses, and thousands of stories to tell.

Of all the books his father brought him throughout his young years, El Cadi liked the ones about history the best, often weaving stories in his head. In his mind, he would compare himself to Simón Bolívar, the great liberator of the 19th century who also arrived in Vieques by accident. On one afternoon he considered wondrous, he witnessed through his binoculars the astounding courage of a man known as Tito Kayak who on his kayak (hence the moniker), faced a large U.S. Navy ship and painted on its hull *Paz para Vieques* in large red letters. From then on, El Cadi jotted down a timeline of the events involving the people of Puerto Rico and the U.S. Navy.

On the same day El Cadi turned fifteen, something tragic occurred in Vieques. The paper's headlines made him wonder if it was an April Fool's joke. He read the headline again: *F-18 U.S. Navy Jet Causes Death of Civilian Guard David Sanes Rodríguez.*

To this day, his father's attitude about this incident still pounds his head. El Cadi called him at work.

"Daddy, did you see the paper?"

"No, what happened?" asked the father, immediately rising from his office chair.

"Did the Marines killed a man?"

"Oh, yes. That was yesterday," said Mr. Richard, sliding his hand through his hair in relief.

"Why didn't you tell me?" asked El Cadi.

"It's not that important! Don't you understand? Besides, that's not our problem. I'm surprised it hasn't happened before. Look, son, the Navy has been training here for years."

"They don't seem to care," added the disappointed teenager. "I'm going out. I want to see what the people have to say about it."

"Cadi, wait. Don't be foolish. That's not our fight. This happens everywhere."

"Daddy, things can't stay like this. That man had a family, maybe even children, friends…" said the infuriated teenager, as he searched for his glasses. "Don't you see how they contaminate the sea? How the fuck can fishermen make a living? Aren't you scared of the bombings? I know I am!"

"Be careful how you talk to me!"

"Let me tell you something, Daddy, the days are numbered for the pilots that play war here. They're going to lynch them. The people here are furious. They have the same fury as Ricky; it's a pent-up hatred that's going to explode any time now."

"Cadi, listen," interrupted Mr. Richard, "You shouldn't leave the house. Ricky can't be left alone. Your brother needs you. Has he had breakfast?" asked the father, deflecting attention away from the conversation.

"I'm not interested in Ricky now! Do you know what he did? I don't know how, but he managed to get his hands on one of my dolls and break it apart. I'm going out. I'll call you later. I need to blow off some steam."

From then on, El Cadi would go out alone each morning for several hours. His compassionate side urged that his father was wrong, and that he hated Ricky. Disappointed with his father's distance and his psychopath brother, El Cadi felt isolated and disjointed. He thought the whole planet was shrouded in gloom.

He exchanged reading for videogames, and he would go out each afternoon to different areas on the island to spy on people. El Cadi always carried binoculars with him, and he would hide in any patch of shade under a tree near Monte David, not far from Carrucho beach. There, sweaty and lustful, he would watch the women and girls joining the protests for peace in their reawakened island. He felt part of the cast in a home movie. From the verdant altar surrounded by virgin green foliage, El Cadi would see nearly every day a crowd marching toward the beaches and surrounding mounds, demanding peace, raising the single-starred Puerto Rican flag with courage, while practicing civil disobedience. He wanted to be there, to join the activists, but he could not risk being seen. If any picture taken of him could reach, within seconds, all corners of the planet, it would certainly reach authorities in Michigan.

El Cadi was not interested in the political figures or celebrities participating in the protests; he was interested in the women. He wanted to do with them what he did to his dolls. He wanted to paint them white.

One day he was stunned by a blond woman who joined the demonstrators demanding that the U.S. Navy leave Vieques. The press identified her as Hillary Clinton. She looked like Dolly. El Cadi believed that her magical touch was what finally made the Navy stop, for once and for all, its bombing practices.

Chapter 15 - The Ceremony

With so much time on his hands, El Cadi was often lost in his memories. He would revisit the past and think about his first years as his brother's custodian. A common tree trunk by the side of the road recalled the thrill of seeing the wooden crate containing his porcelain dolls inside the moving van. He devoted months of preparation to them and only them. He purchased a special cot to place each one on as he fondled and handled them. Possessed by the idea of inflicting agony on Ricky, he embalmed the dolls in front of his brother. El Cadi got new tools for cutting, bending and mutilating the dolls at will. At the end of each ceremony, he would cover the doll in white paper, and using a brush and white glue, he proceeded to embalm her. When they were dry, he would snip off their fingertips as well as a lock of hair and place the pieces in a glass jar identified with the doll's name. He would then hang the embalmed specimens like kites from the basement ceiling. All were hung—some facing up, others facing down—with fishing line wound around their chests, heads, and legs. Since the porcelain sections were heavy, El Cadi took extra care to keep them from falling. He would inspect them every month because the humidity covered them in a green-black mold. El Cadi removed the tape around their eyes, wipe the eyes with a dry cloth and tape them again. Every now and then, like his mother, he would talk to them.

For his very first Christmas in Vieques, El Cadi strung colored lights around all his dolls. The cavern-like basement looked like a parade of whitish scarecrows. He turned on the Christmas lights to see Ricky's reaction.

"Merry Christmas! Do you like it?"

"Very nice, my little Cadi! So childish and such a faggot. You're really screwed up, brother!" cried Ricky furiously, banging his cell bars. "Get me out of here, mother freaky! I want to get out! Tell Richard to come here, I want to talk to him. Tell that good-for-nothing pimp, that Barbarian wannabe says to not be such a coward and to show his face. I have my rights. Get him! Now! Tell him he made a mistake. Tell him you should be the one locked up. You're the one who's crazy."

"Take it easy! If you don't like the lights, that's okay. Then stay there in the dark until New Year's."

El Cadi turned off the lights and slowly walked up the stairs, turning his back on his brother's tirade. He was smiling.

The ceremonial game with the porcelain dolls kept the twins busy until they turned twenty-six. El Cadi did whatever he wanted with the dolls as his brother helplessly watched, unable to touch them. From afar, he took pleasure in watching Ricky pant like a hungry beast, unable to even brush his finger against a strand of artificial hair. He delighted in seeing him look like a caged lion, pacing left to right, his nerves frazzled. He would hear his troubled breathing while kicking his cell bars and growling incoherent gibberish.

El Cadi was already a grown man and was tired of hiding. He had been forced to carry the sins of Ricky, his brother, not just any brother but his identical twin, his living reflection, his mystery and conscience. He was exhausted from a forced solitude that had already lasted fourteen years.

The twins inherited their father's height; Mr. Richard was an outstandingly tall man, with a wrestler's frame and the three had skin so white that the tropical sun gave them hives. The Richards drew attention wherever they went, thanks to the striking red color of their hair. El Cadi groomed the abundant beard framing his face to perfection. He also had small, brown eyes always hidden behind designer sunglasses. But Ricky had no one to flaunt to. His concealed, ruddy good looks and his lack of hygiene made him look more like a vagrant lost in a far and forgotten Normandy.

One boring night, like the one before, El Cadi left La Hueca and landed at Blue Moon Bar. He was so ecstatic over being so close to women, that he became a regular customer. He needed that nightly outing to feel alive. He sniffed an array of feminine scents that reminded him of his porcelain pieces. He then started acquiring a taste for living dolls. He would wait, ever vigilant, for the right time and the right signal to snatch her. He wanted a young woman or—better yet—a girl, to show up like in the movies: easy, perfect, on cue, and easily manipulated. He would try something different now: he would play with a real doll. After all, he learned a few things from the movies he collected and watched repeatedly. Besides, he needed to keep Ricky busy. It was fair and necessary to keep him dead while living in his private cell. Those were the conditions and the pact between El Cadi and his father; that was the fate Ricky determined for himself when he killed his mother. The three breathed the same guilt, the same conspiracy of a death executed during an evil childhood.

But now, El Cadi wanted to live his own life his own way, without caring about his twin brother's tirades and his father's orders.

☼

Throughout the time he lived near the pier in Vieques, Mr. Richard remained apprehensive over his recurring memory of the bathroom incident that changed his life and that of his sons. When his twins came of age, he left them to themselves in that house contrived for them and for obscurity. El Cadi remained in charge of everything. Mr. Richard moved to his business, with a security guard, two menacing mixed-breed dogs, and a gun. He visited his sons once a month, escorted by his dogs. As the years passed his visits became less frequent. He feared that someday, he would encounter another tragedy.

Chapter 16 – Immolation

It was noon, and El Cadi had fulfilled one of his dreams. The so-called Camila awoke to the distant clinking of metal. She thought she was home and that her father was rinsing a bunch of spoons under the faucet. The sound of gushing water persisted. She found it annoying that no one turned off the faucet.

What a waste! How come Mami hasn't yelled at Papi to turn off the faucet? Enough! Thought the girl as she attempted to move, unable to understand why she could not get up.

Her head was throbbing so hard, she could feel swelling from her eyelids to her septum. There was silence, and then an odd whistling made her wonder where she actually was. She moved her eyes under her lids, as if she were dreaming. She tried to open them but was unable to; they were taped shut. She then felt hot spit burning her throat.

El Cadi had prepared her for the ceremony. Another doll, this time a live one, would be initiated before sundown. The so-called Camila had gone missing for twenty-four hours, yet no one actually missed her. Her parents were already used to her long nights out with her classmates. And Las Biz, the gang of smug amorists she aspired joining, thought that she had been lucky enough to catch a man with money. They called that type of guy a *Casanova–zángano,* because his Hugo Boss clothes, his clean, military-style haircut, and his Paco Rabanne's *1 million* scent could ensnare any girl. And by pulling out a wad of cash and a neat row of credit cards, he sent her down the dizzying easy web *round and round she spins* until she stops, catatonic, in his kingdom of gold.

The so-called Camila had not been that lucky. Her legs, arms, neck and waist were cinched to the gurney in the basement. It was the same gurney El Cadi stole from one of the town's ambulances the day Mr. Richard gave him his first all-terrain vehicle at the age of seventeen. It was on that movable altar where he manipulated his dolls-the inanimate and now alive. Next to it, he had a tall table with a white tablecloth on which he placed a tray with the surgical instruments purchased—no questions asked—on eBay. Ever since El Cadi found out how easy it was to buy things online, he navigated the internet for hours, often seeing the strangest, most unbelievable items: everything from specialized nails to materials for assembling a nuclear bomb.

El Cadi did not want to wait for the sleep-inducing powder dropped into the girl's drink to lose effect. He was taking no risks with his first live doll, although he was sorry that he had not enjoyed her longer. He could always find others tomorrow and would become an expert at playing cat and mouse with them. His adrenaline would rise to a hundred, to the max, to total pleasure.

The girl remembered the penultimate episode of her life in fragments. She saw herself dressed in red in her best friend's clothes and recalled segments of a bar in the form of a serpent. She remembered a tall, freckled man who treated her to one, two drinks, and then the lights went out. The so-called Camila started shaking frantically.

Her body did not respond to the commands of her confused mind, and she whimpered softly. She could not cognize anything. She could not even cry if she wanted to. She then tried to yell in a smothered voice, and choked on her own saliva. The gurney wobbled like an agitated sea.

"Do something, idiot! She's going to choke on her vomit!" yelled a frantic Ricky, possessed by his sick desire to take part in the shrouded girl's ceremony. Through the restraining bars of his cell, he wanted to penetrate her with his fingers and fill her face with his cum. Through the bars, he wanted his hands to reach her breasts, to spit between her legs, to lick her lips. He wanted to reduce her to a larva, to see her squirm; he wanted to watch his twin penetrate her and see himself transformed into his brother. He closed his eyes, breathed deeply, and in his mind appeared the image of his mother submerged in the tub. Horrified, he opened his eyes again.

"Cadi, do something or we're going to lose her!" he said gritting his teeth.

"Easy!" snapped his brother, clueless as to what to do.

"Take the gauze out of her mouth!" ordered Ricky.

El Cadi removed the rag from her mouth, just as she vomited a mixture of fluids in vivid hues. The girl gagged, and her body shook from side to side. Her foul-smelling fluids made El Cadi retch, gag, and catch his breath.

"You're such an idiot!" yelled Ricky, turning around to vomit. "I wish the two of you would choke," he thought, holding his nose.

El Cadi grabbed a roll of paper towels and ripped a few sheets to pick up the vomit. He threw them in a garbage bag and carried it up to the house. He needed some fresh air. He took a shower and again dressed in white. He took some disinfectant with him and went down to the basement. He found the gurney turned on its side. The victim was motionless.

"She's unconscious, idiot!" yelled Ricky.

"Dammit!"

"I want her awake. Come on! Get to it, you idiot! Don't let her fall asleep."

El Cadi pulled the gurney up and inspected the victim's binds. He wiped her face with a moist cloth, taped her eyes shut again, and then taped her mouth. Although his fingers were long and thick, they were nimble from playing with his dolls. Without hesitating, he injected Etorphine into the girl's right thigh. He made sure to have the antidote nearby, just in case. Browsing the internet, he saw how several narcotic drugs were used, and decided to buy one for when the desired occasion arose. By immobilizing her, El Cadi would be able to carry out the entire ceremony with no interruptions. His hands shook in fear as they touched a real woman whose body emanated a briny scent. From the short distance, he perceived Ricky's macabre thoughts, beating like a hammer in his head. Their gruesome thoughts bounced back between the two, like a ping-pong ball. Ricky also wanted to possess her, give her one final thrust, but El Cadi was the one enjoying the power he had over the two.

Rape her, kill her, destroy her. Make her squirm, cry in fear; let her die slowly, painfully, letting her feel chills all over her body, let her savor her last breath, put her on a low burner until she goes from life to death.

Those were the thoughts in Ricky's head, passed telepathically to his brother, who carried them out to perfection. Ricky was pleased with how El Cadi cleaned, smoothed, cut, penetrated, and ultimately killed a doll, a true, warm-blooded one with real hair. He was surprised, though when El Cadi gave him the dead girl's tiny panty, as if it were a medal. The prisoner grabbed it with his fingertips, the way a crying baby clutches its hand to fall asleep. He sucked his thumb. He licked his finger and laid down on the futon, his gaze fixed on one of the basement's many dark corners.

El Cadi culminated his desired goal of manipulating a live doll. He was happy he had not given his brother the pleasure of touching her. The girl's rape and torture would remain etched, as on a trophy, in their memories. The so-called Camila was now embalmed. She crossed the threshold of death enshrouded in white, and never once suspected that she had become Las Biz' very first martyr.

Chapter 17 - The Morning Route

The morning was making its way through the eastern coast. The sun's rays were erasing the mist that had settled during the night on the Fajardo town square. At six on the dot, Demetrio was receiving the day's first passengers in the Fajardo public terminal. First came the regular customers: two municipal workers from Carolina, a nurse from the Veteran's Administration hospital, and two students from the University of Puerto Rico. Demetrio called them the *Fantastic Five,* and it was a miracle if he picked them up again, for the afternoon's return trip.

In the following town of Canóvanas, he picked up Margarita, who got off at the next stop eight minutes away. As usual, El Indio got out to help the seventy-something-year-old woman board the van, because the vehicle was too high for her. If he hadn't known her for so many years, he would have thought that she was carrying a pig's head in each of her two bags.

The bags are either heavier than her or she shrinks a centimeter each day, thought El Indio.

"Come right over here, *doña* Margarita, so you won't fall."

"Don't grab me by the waist, because if someone sees us, rumors will start to fly," she said firmly.

El Indio then maneuvered his body to avoid brushing against her and, thus, ruin her reputation. The old Margarita took the van six times a week and always had a story to tell. Yet she left the story hanging, because before she was able to end it, she reached her destination in the Loíza town square. As she exited the van, the woman was aided by two other morning heroes who were about to get on. The brothers Justo and Aníbal opened the two side doors to the van and held Margarita by her forearms. Like a little girl, they lifted her in the air. Not until her feet touched the ground and her bags were securely in her hands did they leave her. She was now ready to take her first steps on the sidewalk. She said goodbye to all on the van and gave them her blessing, leaving them under El Indio's protection.

Demetrio continued his way to Río Grande. The stop there was devoid of passengers and he knew why. The minutes dedicated to the old woman allowed his competitors to go ahead of him and snatch up three or four customers between the towns of Río Grande and Canóvanas.

"It doesn't matter," said Demetrio, chiming. "The last shall be first. I'll catch up."

He was able to step on the gas as he rode between the two towns, but once he reached Carolina, the traffic lights slowed him down again for a few minutes that seemed like hours. He gazed at the rearview mirror inside the van and counted the passengers.

"Seven. Forty dollars. I need three or four passengers more," he figured.

El Indio cut in front of several cars and even drove through three yellow, almost red, traffic lights. He believed that pushing his left arm out of the window gave him the right to swerve in and out of the lanes along the main road, as if his arm were a magic wand that could make everything stop, and clear the way for him. His driving was met with a continuous array of honking horns and insults from the other drivers.

In Carolina—the City of Giants—El Indio regained what he had lost. Three teenage girls with the same uniforms got on. He looked at them with a tinge of nostalgia because they reminded him of his ex-wife, who he loved madly and who made him keep his feet on the ground. He shook his shoulders and greeted them with marked enthusiasm.

"Good morning, my queens! Where are we...?"

The three never lifted their gaze from their phones as they got on and made their way to the only available row of empty seats in the back. They didn't even hear him. Like robots, they got on the van as if pulled in by an invisible cord.

The music everyone heard through the last girls' earphones made for background music in the van. The barrier between them and the rest of the passengers was simply impenetrable.

"As my grandmother used to say, the world is coming to an end," remarked Demetrio to anyone listening.

"If your grandmother said those words and you're repeating them now, it means that you're reaching the age she was when she said them" observed one of the passengers.

"What?" wondered Demetrio, confused with such an entangled sentence.

"Forget it. If I repeat what I said, it won't come out the same."

They all laughed, but the three teens in the back did not even realize that, thanks to them, the world was about to end.

It was seven in the morning—not a minute more, not a minute less—when they reached the bus and public terminal in Río Piedras.

"I need another coffee," said Demetrio under his breath.

Upbeat, with the same good humor as always, El Indio said goodbye to the *Fantastic Five* and the brothers from Loíza, reminding them that he would see them again in the late afternoon for the return trip. It was impossible, however, for the other employees who ended their shifts at four to go back with him. In fact, if he ever saw one of them on the return trip, he understood it could only mean that they've had an emergency.

El Indio closed the van. He greeted the terminal's administrator, who looked at him through the tinted windows of his office. The man, who kept tabs on the vehicles available for service, only lifted his head. Demetrio met with another driver servicing the same route from Fajardo to Río Piedras, and they walked together to the coffee shop on the corner. At that hour in the morning, two women dressed and made up as if for a night of partying, were walking down the middle of the street. They were singing the new bachata by Juan Luis Guerra, swaying their hips in front of the drivers, who looked at them up and down. Demetrio lit a cigarette to ward off the desire pushing through his pants.

"Hey, good looking, can you give me a cigarette?" said one of the women.

"I don't have any. This is an electronic cigarette, and it would be too unsanitary if you took a drag," he lied.

"Liar! C'mon, don't be a bad boy. I need a cigarette before going to bed."

El Indio took a three-second puff and handed it over to the woman.

"Keep it," he said.

"Thanks, sugar daddy!"

The two women continued their way down the street until they disappeared behind the remains of a building abandoned by its owners and by the city. Inside the coffee shop, the drivers chatted about sports, but always ended their conversations on the topic of women. Demetrio struggled against that uncontrollable urge that had destroyed his marriage, and he searched for an excuse to leave the discussion he now found pointless.

He went back to the terminal and opened all his van's doors. He leaned back in the passenger's seat on the right and turned on the battery-operated fan. He dreamed about having a perfect day. The mental stress of getting back to Fajardo before the five o'clock peak time was the only thing that worried him. Demetrio always avoided getting stuck in what he called *the black hole*. Between four and six o'clock in the afternoon, the roads throughout the metropolitan area and the nearby towns were packed and jammed in a gridlock of thousands of cars in all colors. The hours, minutes, seconds spent in that black hole were, he said, a waste of time. Drivers caught on the road during those hours had two options: either they vented their anger by cutting in front of, insulting, and being downright mean to their fellow countrymen, or they could explore the limits of their patience. There was one solution to avoid getting caught in the black hole, and Demetrio prayed for it. He prayed for students to board his van. They normally got out of school earlier than the traffic.

Chapter 18 - Between Dreams

Amid yawns and glances at the paper, El Indio fell asleep in his van. He dreamed a string of blurred visions overlapping the sound of a crying newborn. In his dream, the child's wailing was unbearable, so he went out to his balcony for a smoke. It was getting dark. When he lit the match, he came face to face with the steady gaze of his old neighbor Roque, nicknamed Screw.

"Indio, do you have a driver's license?"

"Yes, why?"

"What do you mean *why?* Look, brother, if you want a job, go to the Public Works Department today and get a public driver's license. I'll rent you the van stuck in my carport and I'll give you the contact number so that you can cover a local route. This is going to help you out, *papi.* I can tell you that your expenses are going to climb. Let's talk tomorrow, okay?"

El Indio remained speechless. He exhaled cigarette smoke in the shape of rings, and mesmerized, his eyes lost in the rings, searched for the answer he needed.

Should I accept his offer? What will we live on? Chloe has just had the baby without even finishing school. And me, I've graduated, but have no job. What do I do? How come Screw knows what I'm going through? Is he an angel? A demon? Do I ask my grandmother? I should apply for college. But we don't even have money for diapers. What if I can work and study? My in-laws are not exactly in the position of being able to feed another mouth. But that's what they're doing. What should I do? Should I try my hand at it? When has a job ever fallen in your lap? If I don't like it, I can always quit. Oh, God, send me a sign.

"God, God," mumbled Demetrio when two teenagers woke him up. "Yeah, what? What is it?" he said confused, sitting upright in the passenger's seat.

"Excuse us, sir. We want to know what the fare to Fajardo is. That man over there told us to come here," said the teenage boy, accompanied by a teenage girl.

El Indio closed his eyes and opened them wide until he came back to reality.

"Five-fifty," managed to say El Indio, his mouth pasty from sleep.

The night's insomnia had left him exhausted. In the background he could hear the other drivers cackling. An echo in the terminal building elongated the laughter. They knew he woke up distracted after his midday naps.

Sons of bitches, was the first thing that crossed his mind.

"Just a minute, please," said the teen boy. He grabbed the girl's hand and the two walked to a bench some ten paces from the van.

Guillermo and Marisol looked uneasily at each other. He pulled out a twenty-dollar bill his father gave him for his birthday. He turned thirteen.

"Marisol, twenty dollars isn't enough for the ferry and back. Maybe we should save some more and try again some other time."

"I've forty. Remember, I told you my grandmother gives us money when we visit. You can't back down now. Please. Look, here's the money," she insisted.

She looked left and right, and then pulled the coin purse from her backpack. She knocked on the wooden bench three times for luck and then opened another backpack pocket to show him a few bottles of water and two green packets of Skittles, the sour kind with tropical fruit flavors.

"My favorite! Thanks baby, our dream of seeing the sunset in Vieques together is about to start. My fearless girl," said Guillermo, giving her a peck on the cheek.

"Don't let me fool you. I'm nervous."

"Me too, but everything will be alright. You'll see. My father says you always have to be positive to jump over every hurdle."

El Indio yawned. He took a deep breath and got out of the van. He stretched his arms, his neck and chest, arching them back. He then glanced at the bench.

Is this a vision or what? Why are these two wandering around like that? I bet I know… they're part of a general plan to get out of school early. With four more, I'll make my day, he thought while scratching his head.

El Indio smoothed his hair back with his fingers and wiped his face and neck with a handkerchief. It was only 1 p.m. He practiced his *good guy* face in front of the van's mirror and approached the kids slowly, but decidedly.

"Uh, look. Where in Fajardo are you going?"

"To the dock for the ferry."

"Are you going to Culebra?"

"No, Vieques."

"I see."

"Do you know when the last ferry leaves?" asked the boy.

"Around four-thirty," lied El Indio, with the idea of leaving early and skirting the traffic jam.

"Will we get there on time?"

"Honestly, kids, if we leave at two or two-thirty, it's likely."

El Indio sensed they were skipping school that day, which amused him because it was not common these days for school kids to cut classes and go out and about. For kids today, playing hooky meant staying locked in a room with hundreds of different video games that could blow one's mind in a virtual world. The two students at the terminal were planning a real escape, and with a few white lies, Demetrio would help them carry out their plan.

It's Romeo and Juliet again, like me and Chloe. Incredible! I should help nurture this romance, the way one places a fallen nest back on a tree, or one carries a newborn for the first time. I pledge before you, invisible spirit wreathing young love, to guide and protect this young couple. First love, the only true, venerated love, will remain forever in this public terminal. This feeling will accompany them to that mystical place in their memory that not even senile oblivion can consume. There's hope even in madness, but the world can't come to an end just yet, thought Demetrio, willing to do anything to preserve what he thought was a lost practice.

"Okay, kids. Since you're both going to the same place, I'll give you a discount. Eight for the two of you."

Guillermo looked at Marisol. She bit her nails and then nodded a few seconds later.

"Okay," said Guillermo, who paid the fare on the spot, leaving no room for changing his mind.

"Thanks," said El Indio, folding the bills into the wad of cash he pulled out from his pants back pocket. "Sit in the back. We'll have to wait for about an hour. With four more, we'll be leaving before two-thirty. I promise."

"Do we have to sit in the back now?" asked Marisol. "It's so hot!"

"Place your backpacks there to reserve your space," said El Indio stretching things a bit. He realized that they had never taken public transportation, and the van hardly ever ran full in the afternoons.

Demetrio thought about how he had lied to them for two good reasons: to complete the day's fares and to serve as a lackey to love, even if he had to disguise his intentions. He would keep his distance, however. People in love need their privacy. He wanted them to encapsulate the time naughty Cupid had planned for them.

"Kids, I'm going to get some coffee. You can go into the van anytime you want."

Demetrio quickened his pace and rubbed his hands together in triumph. He considered them first-class passengers and would even offer them sodas and cookies, but did not want to scare them. He would curb his devilish humor and his sly comments.

"Besides," he whispered with certain mischief, "They must have butterflies in their stomachs."

"Did you turn off your cell phone?" asked Marisol as she sat in the rear of the van.

"As soon as we left school. And how about you?"

"*Mami* took it away from me last night. I texted more than I was supposed to. But I don't care! You should turn yours off completely, because if you feel it vibrating, you'll be tempted to look. At least that's what happens to me and I have to look at it."

"Good idea." Guillermo turned off his phone and slipped it in his backpack.

Chapter 19 - Heading to Fajardo

All was going as planned. Seated in the back row of the van, Marisol and Guillermo waited until four more students showed up. All were college kids who would get off between Carolina and Río Grande. On the rest of the way to Fajardo, Guillermo and Marisol would be accompanied only by El Indio who, unbeknownst to them, would be their guardian.

It was three o'clock. Demetrio was whistling to the romantic melody on the radio. He was happy because he would be returning to Fajardo early, that is, until what happened next. The day's humidity conspired with the dark clouds, and a downpour baptized them just as they were leaving for Trujillo Alto, one of the stops along the route to Fajardo. It seemed as if all the city's parents, grandparents, siblings, aunts, and uncles came out at the same time to pick up their children, grandchildren, siblings, nephews and nieces from school. The result was a traffic jam that embitter even the serenest of drivers. The drivers in traffic maneuvered either to get in or to get out of the jam. It was like seeing the Minotaur's horns in every corner of the labyrinth.

"Two drops, just two drops of rain is what it takes to go from paradise to pandemonium," said El Indio, hitting the van's horn with his fist. "Move it, dammit!" he said, gritting his teeth.

It took him forty minutes to reach Carolina. The bumper-to-bumper cars looked like never-ending chains. El Indio left two students on a corner of the busiest access road in Carolina, and it took him half an hour to cross the town of Carolina, where he left a girl who was able to read while the van was in motion without getting dizzy. "See you tomorrow," said Demetrio, with the sole intention of interrupting her concentration. She did not even bother to answer. It was 4:10 p.m. already, and the penultimate ferry of the day was leaving in twenty minutes.

We won't get there in time, thought El Indio. *I'll have to tell them about their last option.*

El Indio left the last of the college students in Río Grande and turned in his seat to his teen passengers in the back.

"Guys, we're running late for the ferry that's leaving right now, but another one might make it out."

"At what time?" asked Marisol in a childish voice.

"At eight, depending on if whether they were able to fix one of the ferries. Come closer so I won't have to talk loud. I'll give you a couple of options."

Demetrio was concerned over leaving the two kids by themselves in the town of Fajardo. His plan consisted of getting them to the pier for the last ferry of the day and telling them that he would pick them up right there early the following morning to bring them back to Río Piedras. But he was not willing to leave them there by themselves for several hours in a place they had never visited without even knowing whether they would be able to get on a boat at all. The thrill of romance was quickly evaporating.

Marisol and Guillermo grabbed their backpacks and sat in the first row. They held hands while holding on to the back of the driver's seat. Demetrio noticed their interlaced fingers. They were still so small. It was then when he realized they were placing their entire trust in him. He had to level with them.

"Look, I'm going to be honest. I don't want to leave you in town or near the pier by yourselves, because you aren't familiar with the area. Do you understand?"

The two teenagers nodded.

"I can't assure you that another ferry will leave at night. That's the whole truth. If you allow me to, I'll give you some advice. One: you could go back to Río Piedras with another driver who's leaving in about an hour. Or two: you can go to Vieques with a fisherman friend of mine. You've got five minutes to decide. We should be reaching Fajardo in about forty-five minutes, depending on traffic."

Marisol's eyes welled with tears and she leaned her head against Guillermo's shoulder.

"Baby, don't get that way. What do you want to do? I'll do whatever it is you want."

"I'm afraid," said Marisol.

"So, we'll go back home."

"No," she said getting up with renewed energy. "We're this close. Everything will be alright. Think like your father. Okay? We'll go on the boat with the fisherman."

Guillermo sighed in disappointment. His hands were shaking, and he started sweating. He felt guilty for telling her about Vieques and giving in to the plan from the beginning. He felt manipulated by a childish whim, but at the same time he liked the idea of being with Marisol and pleasing her. In his eyes, she was so brave and beautiful. No one compared to his *baby,* but his intuition was telling him to not go on with it.

"So what'll it be, kids?"

"We're going to Vieques," said Marisol.

El Indio and Guillermo exchanged glances through the rearview mirror. There was a moment of uncomfortable silence, but the driver quickly pulled out his tourist guide hat from the glove compartment. It was white with red letters that read: *Puerto Rico Does It Better.*

"I'll bet you can't guess what the majestic mountain on your right is. It's El Yunque. Did you know that it's the only tropical rain forest in the U.S. forest system?" El Indio cleared his throat and he enthusiastically continued: "Legend has it that on that sacred mountain lived the good spirit of Yuquiyú, the protector of our Taíno people. I think it's still there, and when there's a hurricane headed our way, Yuquiyú pulls out his gigantic fan and blows it away. Guys, I think your next visit should be here, in Luquillo. Aside from getting some exercise, it's a lovely climb up to the highest peak, where you can feel the soft drizzle from the clouds."

Chapter 20 - Ángel, The Fisherman

El Indio called an old fisherman friend he had met in a bar near the pier in Fajardo. Together they would share a few beers and life stories. Ángel lived in Vieques, and each day from Monday to Friday, he sailed with his daughters to Fajardo and back. His daughters preferred studying in the bilingual school in Fajardo, even if it meant more of a hassle and getting up very early. Like most of the young people from Vieques, his two daughters were planning on moving to the island of Puerto Rico, or even outside the island.

Yet the hidden truth about the fisherman's daily sailing would surface when he and his friends, amid smoke and drinks, confided their secrets to one another. Ángel and his wife feared that their daughters might meet some guy and get pregnant if they stayed in Vieques. Demetrio told him however, that even the purest, most hidden desires couldn't be controlled, especially the ones that make people feel alive. He hoped the best for Ángel and his wife.

"Ángel, my friend, how are you?"

"Fine, Indio, how about you?"

"I'm great. Look, I need a favor. Are you still in Fajardo?"

"Yes, what happened?"

"I've got two passengers that need to get to Vieques. Is that possible?"

"Are they heavy?"

"Not even a hundred pounds wet each," chuckled Demetrio.

"Okay. Look for me at the pier in about half an hour? Okay?"

"Sure, thanks. I owe you one," said El Indio, relieved.

Demetrio waited next to his two young passengers by the pier in Fajardo for Ángel and his daughters. When he saw the three walking towards him, he warned Guillermo and Marisol to be careful in Vieques, to stay together at all times, and to call him if there was an emergency. He offered to take them back to Río Piedras at any time. The kids thanked Demetrio and jotted down his number in one of their school notebooks. Guillermo put the piece of paper in his pants pocket.

"But where are my manners!" said Demetrio. "We've been together for nearly three hours and I don't even know your names."

"I'm Guillermo and she's Marisol."

"Pleased to meet you. I'm Demetrio, but everyone calls me El Indio. Remember, give me a call to pick you up tomorrow."

"Okay," said the two.

El Indio introduced everyone and signaled for Ángel to call him when they got to Vieques. Ángel nodded. The two lovebirds held hands, went aboard the boat, and let go of each other only to wave at Demetrio.

Chapter 21 - Heading to Vieques

It was sundown. Seated on the boat, all observed the sunset in silence. That was the plan; to see the sunset in each other's arms.

"When the sun comes up or goes down along that horizontal line," said Ángel pointing to the west, "even the seagulls stay quiet. If they're quite enough, they can feel the earth move."

The sea was placid, and they sailed windward swiftly to Vieques. Marisol enjoyed the short boat ride. She would close her eyes and lift her head to breath in the salty air. But Guillermo was nervous, on alert, and he held on to the boat when it rocked a little too roughly. He felt queasy. Marisol caressed his hair and he, surrendering to her caresses, closed his eyes.

They reached the Isabel Segunda pier at 6:30.

"We're here!" announced the fisherman, and one of his daughters uncoiled the rope at her feet to tie the boat to one of the pier's moorings. The other daughter looked at the two teenagers.

"Where are you going?" she asked them.

"To my aunt's house," lied Guillermo.

"If you want to, I can accompany you so you won't be by yourselves. Where does she live?" asked the daughter.

"Uh, I have the address in one of my notebooks, but don't worry," he said self-assuredly. Marisol squeezed his hand.

"We're going to Esperanza, where most of the people here live. Does that sound familiar?"

"Yes, it's right there. Would you take us?"

"Of course," said the young woman who, like her parents and grandparents before her, was accustomed to helping people.

The five went up the street from the pier to a busier area. Not five minutes had passed when an acquaintance of Ángel stopped mid-street and offered them a ride in his old public van, already streaked in three tones of blue and bashed in on its four corners. He picked them all up. The people on Isla Nena are always willing to lend a helping hand to both the people they know and to those they don't. They say those are the blessings of living in a small town.

Chapter 22 - Mari Olga

From inside the van, Demetrio saw the fishing boat containing its few passengers, get smaller as it sailed away. The passengers stopped waving their restless goodbyes and were now drawn to the dark green island in the distance in front of them. The wind was pushing two seagulls as they glided no higher than twenty feet over the water. They confidently extended their wings, adroitly playing with the castles in the air.

El Indio watched them with an unlit cigarette between his lips. He lit the cigarette and took a good, long puff. In a small, hidden corner somewhere inside, Demetrio slightly resented that he was no longer important to the kids. It bothered him that his role as the lackey of love in Marisol and Guillermo's romance was over. He had a hunch that there would be a problem at some point. So, he looked at his ring with the Indian head, spit on it, and buffed it on his pants. Speaking in a strange dialect, he counted the feathers on the Indian's headdress, and made the sign of the cross, as if wishing to ward off his bad thoughts with that small ritual.

He took another puff and forced himself to switch to another thought. He sighed like a young lover and whispered a woman's name: Mari Olga. Infected with the romance in the day's air, he thought it was time for another chance at love. All these lonely nights are pathetic. He would do something out of the ordinary and invite his neighbor out. He put his hand to his chest, smiled, and exhaled with a renewed air.

Oh, Indio, you lovesick man. When are you going to take love seriously? he thought.

☼

Mari Olga, a fifty-something-year-old woman, had a silky, coffee-and-cream colored complexion that made her look much younger than her years. She had a plump face, a small nose, and a roguish sparkle in her eyes. She lived across from the Fajardo town square. Each afternoon she sat behind the tall gate on her front porch, where Demetrio admired her from his second-story apartment. Mari Olga rocked in her rocking chair, while listening to romantic *trio* music on a portable radio she hung inside a macramé basket. She was mesmerized by the music and sported a perpetual smile, like the mysterious Mona Lisa. She greeted the people she knew by lifting her hand as they passed by. Seated there, she waited for the night to fall until some inebriated being would stumble by, upsetting her with rude catcalls. She would slam the door behind her, announcing to the neighborhood that she was done for the evening. She also cast side-glances to Demetrio. She had the impression that he was a good-natured, polite man who carried himself with honest grace. He had a certain air that reminded her of her grandfather, whom she secretly admired because, even though he was a quiet man, he was a handful. A line of women followed him throughout his life, even to his funeral.

♥

Demetrio, still elated by the breeze on the pier, had Mari Olga on his mind, and he thought about her well-formed legs and her bare feet on the porch floor. Each afternoon he watched her from his bedroom window. It was hard for him to be alone after so many years of marriage. Like most people in the square he, too, greeted her, after he had left his van at the Fajardo terminal. From there, he walked briskly, with the lilt he was known for, going up and down the town's narrow streets. Before reaching Mari Olga's house, he slowed down. He would stop before her porch, greet her, and then cross the one-way street. He would then enter the old, three-story house where he lived, and he stayed there until the following morning when he commenced his regular routine as a public driver.

The first time El Indio noticed her was when he heard the music coming from her front porch. He was surprised to see a woman of her age enjoying the melodies of yore, which were the ones he also enjoyed. It was the music his grandmother listened to more than half a century earlier. *What better way to take the next step than to talk about music,* thought El Indio. Their cordial greetings stretched into small talk about music, the weather, higher electrical bills, and a story or two about his daily drive to Río Piedras. A month later, he offered to drive her—free of charge—to San Juan whenever she needed to go. Demetrio did not want to hurry into courtship. He would keep his fondness for her to himself until he found out whether she was free. Being involved in a romantic triangle, or with even more people, had brought him a share of problems in the past. Those fifteen minutes of pleasure caused eternal regrets beyond repair. Which was why he was satisfied for now with merely watching her from afar, although he had no idea what she did during the day. In one of those brief conversations, El Indio noticed a little flirting on her part. Perhaps he was misinterpreting her. He was not sure, so he thought it was best to wait for another direct cue. But on that evening, inspired by the romantic charm of the two teenagers, Demetrio decided it was time to take the plunge. The time for love was now, and he wanted to explore a passion he believed lay dormant.

Would she be on her porch? Today is the day! I'll invite her out this very evening, he thought, excited.

The coastal breeze slightly shook his van, making him believe he was being visited by an obscure spirit. He fretted, again, over Marisol and Guillermo.

"They must be reaching Vieques by now. Did I do the right thing in bringing them?" he added to his woes, whispering:

"You're such an idiot! First you encourage them, and now you're a jerk! Get with it!"

Demetrio tried to turn on his vehicle. The motor remained silent. He tried again...and nothing. He punched the steering wheel and tried one more time, in vain. He got out and searched for some pliers in the back, opened the hood, and tapped the battery a few times. He turned the key again. Perhaps it was the engine since he had recently installed a new battery. Neither with punches nor insults did the van respond.

"I have no intention of fiddling with the car now, much less smearing grease all over my clothes. Dammit! What do I do now?" he said furiously, and he went inside the van again, slamming the door so hard that the whole vehicle shook. With his evening plans thwarted, El Indio became distracted again, watching the poised seagulls. He was very easily distracted. Exhausted from lack of sleep, he closed his eyes for only a moment and dozed off for about twenty seconds. He suddenly opened his eyes in horror. In those few seconds, he had a hair-raising dream of a girl completely painted in white, her eyes wide open, like fish's eyes. With his heart banging, he grabbed his chest, and a bee came buzzing in through the partially opened passenger-side window. It looked like a small rocket aiming for his nose. The bee buzzed stubbornly next to him.

"Goodness, *abuelita*, you're going to scare me to death!" he exclaimed startled, and he got out of the van to avoid being stung. After his grandmother died some thirty years earlier, a spiritualist assured him that she had reincarnated into a bee and would watch over him for as long as he lived. In fact, a bee would appear whenever he became distracted and could not make up his mind about an issue. He believed the bee was his grandmother looking after him.

"Okay, I get it! It's about those kids, right? But I have to do something first before I go out to Vieques," he said grumpily, and pulled out a comb to tame his wayward locks.

Once outside his van, a swirling wind pulled out the pages from a newspaper on the ground, and they disbanded like a flock of fleeing pigeons. The wind pushed one of the pages between Demetrio's feet. When he picked it up, he saw for the second time that day the headline he read in the morning: *Another girl goes missing in Vieques.* He threw the paper away in disgust. He looked around and making sure no one saw him, put the van key on the front left tire.

"I shouldn't take any risks with my little van," he said after pushing down the hood and locking all the doors.

Demetrio knew very well that no vehicle was safe on that solitary pier. He wiped off his sweat with a handkerchief and walked briskly towards a small business he saw at a distance. On the way, he pulled out his phone and spoke to the terminal office, asking them to call a tow truck. He mentioned where the key was. Although the tow truck would be there in less than half an hour, he needed every minute to carry out his plan. Having his van out of service meant that the next day would be an unproductive one. Immediately, he began regretting the decisions made throughout the day, but a persistent buzzing from afar reminded him of his new plan to finish what he started. He reached the business, which after five was disguised as a bar. In a corner in the back, two bald men with tank tops and protruding bellies were sharing the start of the evening with beers and cigars. El Indio glanced at them, but they were unrecognizable under the smoke. He greeted them with a slight nod of the head. He then leaned over the counter looking for the person in charge who was hidden behind a tattered, half-open curtain. He, too, was smoking.

"*Jefe*, my van broke down right there on the pier," pointed El Indio, "and the tow truck is on its way. If you can, keep an eye on it, you know, just in case. Can you, my friend?"

The man nodded. Demetrio pulled out some change from his pocket, gave it a slight smack on the bar, and headed to town in the same brisk pace.

If I were to put all of my feelings in a blender, I would become the Tasmanian Devil, he thought as he made his way up a street with concrete houses in bright hues, protected by iron bars over the window.

Although he was nervous about the kids, El Indio was also anxious to see Mari Olga seated on her porch and ask her out, with no qualms whatsoever. He was also concerned about leaving the van untended at the pier. But again, his mind went back to the teenagers in Vieques. He pulled out his cell phone and texted Ángel, inquiring about them. It took the fisherman less than ten seconds to reply: *They are on their way to their aunt's house in Esperanza.*

What aunt? Dammit! These kids! Why did I bring them here? Why am a such a ...! And to think that my grandmother gave me a few bops on the head so that I would mind my own business, said El Indio grimacing as he scratched his head.

Without realizing it, Demetrio was already on the corner heading to Mari Olga's house. He paused, pulled out his comb and swept back his hair, now moist with sweat. He was invigorated and smoothed his eyebrows with his index fingers, and changed his attitude from glum to carefree and charming. He was accustomed to amorous encounters—as well as decent and indecent proposals—with a history of women under his belt. But this time he feared a *"no"* from Mari Olga. He feared the idiotic expression on his face if she refused. He would not know how to proceed afterwards. He was afraid of the future; of passing by her house the following day and facing a rejection that would hurt his old heart. Debating whether to settle for daily chitchat or submit to a possible silent snub was eating him up inside.

What do I do? he wondered.

The sound trio music announced his proximity to her home. Trio Vegabajeño was interpreting a song about torment and suffering. Five paces more and he would be right in front of the so-admired neighbor. His skipping heart beat reminded him of what he felt when he gave his eighth-grade teacher his first love poem. He sensed the anxiety on his skin, the moister from sweat, and his churning stomach. Being out of practice irked him. At last, he turned the corner and was there in front of her porch. He thought he saw a vision. When he saw her dressed in white, El Indio grabbed the gates with both hands to avoid the embarrassment of falling in front of her. A chill went down his spine and paralyzed him. He felt his legs firm on the sidewalk again once she spoke.

"Demetrio, is there something wrong?"

El Indio closed his mouth and swallowed hard. His mind was in solitary confinement. He took longer than he wanted to answer.

"What's up? No, nothing's wrong."

Just as he was about to engage in conversation, the radio station interrupted its programming. She lifted her index finger and pointed it to her left ear. Demetrio followed her unspoken order to keep quiet. He needed that moment to sort his words and place them in order.

The radio announced that Marisol and Guillermo were missing. El Indio turned around to see the statue on the square.

"Those kids again!" he whispered.

"Did you hear that?" said Mari Olga.

"Yes," replied El Indio, staring at the gigantic statue, adding, "And I know where they are."

"What did you say?" she asked, standing closer to him behind the gates, with her hands on her hips.

"I picked them up in Río Piedras and now they're in Vieques," said Demetrio, startled upon seeing her so close.

"Oh, come on! I'm calling 911."

"No, no wait. They went on a boat with a friend of mine and should be fine. What probably happened is that they did not have permission from their parents. Yes, that's it," he said firmly, as if attempting to excuse himself from his anxiety and appease her sense of urgency.

"Excuse me, Demetrio, but that's wrong. Didn't you hear that they're only twelve and thirteen. They're babies."

"I was thinking about going…"

"Going where? To look for them?" asked Mari Olga confused.

"I know it sounds funny, but yes. But that's another story. You see, the reason I stopped by was to ask you a bold question," said Demetrio, gazing at the floor shyly.

"Well, tell me!" she insisted, furrowing her brow.

"Would you come with me to look for them?" he asked, fearing her reply.

"To Vieques. *Ay bendito,* you poor thing! I can't. I'm taking care of my mother, and she's very old. But you know what? I love the idea. I'm so close to Isla Nena, and I haven't seen it in years. Demetrio, please go find those kids right now. They must be on the beach somewhere. Don't waste any more time. You can still catch the last ferry out. In any case, I'll call the authorities to let them know. We'll talk tomorrow."

El Indio smiled in surprise, with a certain hopeful disappointment. He nervously pulled out his handkerchief and wiped his forehead.

"You're right. Tomorrow! How about I pick you up at this same time? We can have some coffee, or ice cream, whatever you want," said Demetrio casually, even though he was trembling inside.

"Okay," she said without much emotion, as if she were accustomed to being asked out. "I'll make arrangements so someone stays with *Mami*. But go on, already. Hurry up!"

"Yes!" he answered striding down the street. He glanced at his watch and ran to catch the ferry in time.

Chapter 23 - The Last Ferry of the Day

El Indio reached the pier exhausted. The last ferry of the day was leaving in five minutes. There were two ticket lines; one for passengers bound for Culebra, and the other for the ones bound for Vieques. Only a single ticket vendor serviced the two lines behind a window. There were few tourists going on the ferry that evening, and the residents of both islands municipalities usually bought their return tickets in the morning. The passengers bound for Vieques were going home tired after a long day.

"Two twenty-five," said the young man behind the ticket window.

Demetrio showed him his driver's license and his tour-guide ID.

"A ticket to Vieques and I think I don't have pay the fare," he said, tapping his ID card with his index finger.

"Sir, could you tell me where your group is?"

"What group?"

"I can give you a courtesy pass only if you're going as a tour guide. But it's obvious that…"

"Oh, I see! Look, it's just that I'm on my way to Vieques to pick up the group, you know," said Demetrio scratching his head. "I had to come back because of an emergency, but I'll be back here tomorrow with my group. You know?"

The employee stared at him annoyed, tapping the counter with his fingers. His mind ran through the entire collection of excuses and lies the passengers sometimes told him. In a patient tone, as if speaking to a child, he added: "Do you by chance have this morning's canceled ticket?"

"Oh, *caramba*! Let me see," answered Demetrio. He searched all his pants pockets, grinning with a sorry expression. "No, my friend, what a shame!"

"Here's a courtesy ticket, but you have to get the return ticket in Vieques."

"No problem. Of course. Thank you very much. I'll see you early tomorrow. You'll see."

The ticket seller ignored El Indio's small chitchat and kept on reading his book. Demetrio entered the terminal and looked for a seat. Everything was taken. When he saw the Vieques ferry's crew climb down the white, two-level ferry to begin the boarding process, he quickened his pace and approached the middle of the line. The crewmen, dressed in the official port authority uniform, cupped his hands over his mouth, forming a megaphone, and yelled: "Vieques."

The people in line picked up their bags and backpacks and crowded the exit to the platform. Demetrio looked at each person, hoping to find a familiar face, perhaps one of his own passengers whose name he did not know. He did not recognize anyone. He approached a woman with an embittered expression, but she looked at him and without beating around the bush, very clearly said: "Not here, mister. Go to the back of the line!"

El Indio looked back and saw that the others in line were watching him. They were very aware of all the ruses people use to cut lines. Demetrio lowered his head, put his hands in his pockets and smiled in embarrassment. From the back of the line, he stuck his head out to the left and then to the right and wondered why it wasn't moving. He pulled out his comb and stayed amused with his hair until he finally handed over his ticket.

They're not from here, but from where else could they be? Ten thousand Boricuas separated by the sea, thought El

Indio, and he pulled out his small notebook to jot those words down. *That would make for a good song.*

It was at that moment that another bee buzzed right in front of his nose. *I'm on my way, abuelita, on my way,* he thought, brushing the bee aside. El Indio again worried about Marisol and Guillermo.

Am I an accomplice in a tragedy? This is going to cause me problems. I'll lose my job. You're such a coward, Demetrio. What will happen if I go to jail? What will I tell Mari Olga? I guess I'll have time to think and write in jail. Yes, I'll write. But will she wait for me? This is so stupid!

Demetrio climbed up to the boat's second level. He leaned against the railing and crossed his arms over his chest. He then stretched his legs and put his hands in his pockets. He was restless like a whirlwind. He turned around with a dull expression while looking at the passengers still on the platform. He admitted that patience was not a virtue of his, and he anxiously tapped the handrail, as if it was a pair of congas. He stayed hopeful about Mari Olga's reply.

The ferry's horn startled him. The gusts of wind tousled his hair; some of his locks haphazardly thrashed his cheeks, forcing him to squint. He turned around again. He was cold. Afraid of an unknown outcome resulting from this unusual day, he turned his back to Vieques and focused on the beams lighting the Fajardo pier, as if he wished to remain on the main island.

"Let's go!" yelled the crewman after untying the ropes binding the ferry to the platform.

Chapter 24 – Stalking

It was a clear night in Vieques. The ferry's horn interrupted the melodic flow of the sea on the sand, announcing the arrival of the last of the Isla Nena returning residents. The dock's attendant put away his cell phone that was keeping him amused and tied a rope around the wooden stump. The ferry's passengers exited exhausted and drowsy. They were like a handful of prodigal sons finally setting foot at the end of the day on their beloved land. Demetrio exited with another passenger, as if he had known him all his life. As soon as he stepped on Vieques, he sighed in relief. He believed his grandmother would be more at ease.

From the car rental business near the pier, El Cadi was stalking people through his binoculars. Leaning back in his car seat, he watched the women getting off the last ferry of the day. Nothing caught his eye. It was a little after 8 p.m. and he was hungry. It was past his strict dinner time. He turned on the car and headed to the Blue Moon. When he reached Esperanza, he slowed down. He leered at each female body he saw. With this free hand, he stroked his penis over his pants. He prayed for a breeze to lift their short skirts. He continuously licked his lips. Couples, families, and friends were dining throughout that touristic area and strolling with piña coladas in hand along the boardwalk. His cat's eye landed on an unusual couple.

Marisol and Guillermo, with only hours in Vieques, were holding hands. They were especially discernable because their school uniforms were different from the usual ones in

Vieques. No adults were with them. Every so often, Marisol pulled out a piece of candy from her small, green bag and with child-like playfulness, place it on the boy's lips. They laughed delightfully, and lightly ambled about, as if walking on air. With their arms around each other, they discovered the tropical charms of this small island in a space devoid of time and worries. Being together amid so much natural beauty erased all the afternoon's apprehensions.

A little doll, thought El Cadi, *so fragile, so innocent, so mine.*

El Cadi parked his car as his eyes stayed on them. His guts were talking to him. He got out and followed them. The teens sat on a bench in the promenade and searched in one of their backpacks. Marisol pulled out her coin purse and they walked to a sandwich truck parked in front of an empty store with a *For Sale* sign.

"A *tripleta*, please," said Guillermo.

El Cadi approached and waited right behind the girl. He was mesmerized by the copper highlights in Marisol's long and abundant hair. He wanted to touch her hair, but refrained. He stood two spaces behind the youngsters. When they sensed his presence, they turned around. El Cadi immediately gazed at the hand-written menu on a small chalkboard.

"What will you have to drink?" asked the cook.

"Nothing, we're fine," said Marisol, patting her backpack to remind Guillermo that she brought water.

"I'll call you in a minute. And you, sir, what would you like?" he asked El Cadi while throwing slices of ham, steak, and pull pork on the hot grill.

"Two rare skirt steaks with french fries."

"Rare? My friend, that's almost raw. You sure?"

"Yes. The people here have no idea how to eat meat," replied El Cadi adding: "I want two Coca-Colas and a lemonade."

"Oh. I'm out of lemonade. I've orange, passion fruit, guava, and acerola juices." The cook looked in the direction of the two teens and cried, "Tripleta, ready!"

"Passion fruit then, and I want it now," demanded El Cadi.

"Sure, mister."

Guillermo paid and walked with his girlfriend down the sidewalk. They vanished, as if swallowed by the nocturnal landscape. El Cadi noticed where they went. The two went down the pebbled walkway leading to the beach and sat under some palm trees, leaning against their trunks. El Cadi took the passion fruit juice from the counter and turned around. He pulled a small bag from his pocket containing enough powder to knock out a dozen horses. He sprinkled a pinch of the powder into the juice and stirred it with two straws. He told the cook he would be back soon and headed to the beach. From afar, he watched them eat. He silently approached them and interrupted only when he was just a few feet away.

"Hi, don't be alarmed. This is from the guy in the sandwich truck. He said you left it on the counter," said El Cadi clearing his throat and extending the drink with his arm.

The kids stepped back.

"We didn't order any juice," answered Guillermo sternly.

"Yes, I asked for it. You were distracted and didn't notice," interrupted Marisol.

"Really?" asked Guillermo, noticing Marisol winking at him.

"The cook looked for you and didn't see you, so he left it on the counter. If you don't want it…"

"Sure we do. Thank you," said Marisol, taking the plastic cup.

"You're welcome. Enjoy your meal," said El Cadi, keeping his eyes on the girl. He then left.

"We got a free juice! Mmm! I love passion fruit!" said Marisol, immediately drinking the juice.

"Wait, Baby! What are you doing? You don't know if..."

"What are you talking about?" said Marisol. "You, yourself said that the people here are very friendly. Go ahead. Try it. It's really delicious. I was actually craving something sweet to drink."

"I'd rather have water," said Guillermo flatly.

Marisol ate her half of the sandwich and drank the juice. Guillermo was full and saved the rest in his backpack for the following day. He had some water. He thought of what had just happened, and his parents came to mind. He recalled the uncomfortable silence at home after an argument. His father was always quiet, while his mother filled the void with some trivial topic. That is what happened under those palm trees that same moment. Marisol leaned against him and pointed to the stars.

"Look, the big dipper! Do you see it?"

He remained silent. With his free hand, he caressed one of the girl's long curls. They gazed at the stars for a while. Then looked at each other. They remained still and silent for a few seconds, until he, without hesitating, pulled up her chin and drew his face closer, then to his lips. Then and there, the two found their very first tender kiss. At such a young age they understood how perfect love was. That first kiss came at the right place, but at the wrong time, because he would have wanted it to happen as the sun was setting. From then on, their kisses were infinite. Marisol opened her eyes to make sure she wasn't dreaming. His thirst for her was quenched by the passion of her lips. The crashing waves joined their mischievousness complicity with their heartbeats. Marisol let him take the lead in savoring her new flavors, and she moaned with pleasure. Guillermo passionately held her and kissed her neck. She lay on her back, limp, like a ragdoll.

"Baby, I love you," whispered Guillermo, again kissing her lips.

Suddenly, she stopped moving. He said her name several times, shook her softly, and again caressed her hair, but Marisol's thin body did not respond. Guillermo got up and put his hands on his head. He looked everywhere, thinking how the moon was the only witness to his despair. However, El Cadi's shadow lurked behind the thick bushes. With a thin toothpick, he picked the meat leftover in his teeth and gums. His gums bled. He enjoyed sucking on the warm, salty blood. His mind was filled with obscenity and wished he was in Guillermo's place. Hunched like a waiting falcon, El Cadi watched something he had never seen before. A fine sliver of moon light illuminated him as the wretched degenerate he is.

I want to be loved that way, even if it means killing her, and cutting her up afterwards.

Chapter 25 – Despair

On his way to Vieques, Demetrio befriended another passenger who turned out to be Ángel's second cousin. Without even setting foot on the pier, he already had a ride to Esperanza. El Indio knew the kids were there because Ángel had texted him.

Demetrio walked along the streets bursting with bars, restaurants, and hotels under construction. He peered through the display windows yet saw no familiar faces. He crossed the street for a smoke to ward off his hunger. He looked everywhere, hoping to find Guillermo and Marisol's turquoise school uniform. After searching for about half an hour, he spotted that blue he so desperately looked for. It was Guillermo, but he was by himself. Guillermo walked quickly, grabbing his head and looked everywhere. In a flash, the boy was at the sandwich truck.

Demetrio put out his nearly new cigarette and approached him. The boy waved his hands as spoke to the cook.

"Guillermo!" yelled El Indio.

The teenager ran to him in despair. The boy was ruffled and pale.

"Mr. Driver, it's so good to see you. Look, my girlfriend is unconscious; she fainted in my arms and I don't know what to do!" exclaimed Guillermo, grabbing El Indio by the arm and leading him to the beach.

"Is she diabetic?" asked El Indio.

"I don't know. I don't think so. I guess she would have told me so. Come, please!"

"We have to take her to the hospital," added Demetrio.

"I know, but I can't carry her by myself. Follow me!" cried the boy, going down the sand dunes toward a line of palm trees.

Guillermo tried to hurry, but the soft sand hampered his steps. Demetrio followed, but fell behind ten paces; the years made him less nimble. The boy identified the palm trees by the backpacks leaning against them. But then, his despair grew, and he went slipping in circles around the trees. He looked like a crab burrowing into the sand.

"Where is she?" yelled Guillermo.

"You tell me."

"She was right here, next to the backpacks!"

"Oh my God. It can't be," added El Indio, scratching his head.

"Marisol!" they yelled a dozen times in all directions.

"Son, wait. We have to calm down. Let's see," said El Indio.

Guillermo started to cry, Demetrio shook him by the shoulders, and said,

"Look, this is serious. Try to remember everything that happened."

Amid tears and desperate gestures, Guillermo told him that they rode with Ángel to Esperanza and then said goodbye, because he wanted to be alone with Marisol. They bought food at the sandwich truck and then went over to the beach under the palm trees. Guillermo thought a little longer and suddenly exclaimed,

"I know!"

"What?" asked El Indio.

"The juice guy!"

"What juice? What guy? What do you mean?"

"Follow me," begged Guillermo.

They each grabbed a backpack and ran back to the food truck. Panting, the boy asked the cook if he had sent a passion fruit juice to them with the red-haired man standing in line behind them.

"Absolutely not! You two only ordered a *tripleta* sandwich. Don't you remember?" said the cook.

"You see!" said Guillermo to Demetrio. "Excuse me sir, but did that man also order a passion fruit juice?"

"Yes, and I found it odd, but since there's always a glutton here and there, even in the Lord village…"

"My fellow Christian, tell me what that man ordered to drink," implored Demetrio, while trying light another cigarette.

"Two Cokes and a passion fruit juice. Why? Did something happen?"

"Yes, well, I think he kidnapped my girlfriend," said Guillermo, collapsing into a folding chair to cry and hiding his face inside his shirt.

"What? What do you mean?"

"Do you know who he is?" asked Demetrio.

"He and his father have lived here for quite a few years. You know, foreigners who set up a business to live in so-called paradise."

"Do you know his name? Where he lives? Look, this is an emergency."

"Well, they call them the Vikings. The man has a car rental place by the pier and his son, the one who was here, lives, I think, in an *armored* house in La Hueca."

"What do you mean an *armored* house?" said El Indio loudly.

"Well, the house is surrounded by an electrical fence and no one has ever been inside, according to what people say."

"Oh, blessed be thy name of Jesus!" whispered El Indio. He finally lit his cigarette and scratched his head while in thought.

"What do we do?" asked Guillermo still crying.

"Look, forgive me for butting in," said the cook, "but someone in my family is on the police force and…"

"Well, call him right now!" ordered El Indio, taking a drag and squinting his eyes. "Tell him what happened. Tell him a girl has gone missing. Her name is Marisol. What is her last name?"

"Vargas Rosa," answered the boy, his head now hanging as he dried his eyes with his shirt.

"Did you hear that? Write it down on your blackboard. It's a life-or-death matter."

"Will do," said the cook, wiping his hands on his apron before picking up his cell phone.

As the cook explained the situation to the officer on the phone, Demetrio and Guillermo walked a few paces over to the sidewalk.

"What do we do now?" asked the boy. He walked to the middle of the street. He still had hope and was in denial. Each time the door to a nearby business opened, he expected to see Marisol coming out sunny and smiling as usual, as if she was playing hide-and-seek.

"Maybe she's in the bathroom," whispered Guillermo, still looking everywhere.

"Wake up, son! We need a car!" said El Indio, who asked the cook for some water.

"Do you want some passion fruit juice? It's good for high blood pressure."

"What did the officer say?"

"That they're going to patrol La Hueca. But you two have to go to the police station to request an investigation and file some sort of report…, what was it that he said? Right, you need a search warrant."

"Look, Guillermo, you have to do this on your own," whispered El Indio. He cleared his voice and added in a sorry tone; "the thing is, if I get involved in all of this, I have a lot to lose. Since you two are minors, I shouldn't have let you in my van and taken you so far away from home. Do you understand? I could go to jail for this."

The boy stared at him in disappointment and hung his head. The cook, meanwhile, was now nervous and attempted to hear what they discussed until he eventually interrupted,

"Look, my friends, I don't think I'll sell much more tonight. If you want, I'll take you to the police station. It's not far from here."

"Please, take us," said El Indio without hesitation.

The cook hurriedly closed his kitchen and put everything away as Guillermo sat on the sidewalk, staring at a rock. His expression turned flat and he was stupefied by how quickly tears evaporated in the tropical breeze.

El Indio, on the other hand, was exasperated by the slow pace of time. He crossed the street to smoke his last cigarette and called the fisherman. Ángel did not answer. With each puff, Demetrio stared deeper into the sea's darkness. He hadn't remembered having so many issues since his divorce. First and foremost, he had to find Marisol. Second, he had to explain to the authorities his role in all of this. He blamed himself for following a very personal romantic thread, which was now an entangled mess. All in all, he would help Guillermo, but would keep his distance.

The cook honked his horn. Neither heard when their good Samaritan started the motor and pulled into the street. The two ran and got in. Demetrio sat in the front seat and Guillermo sat in the back on a cooler, his legs sliding on the greasy floor with the scraps of meat, wilted lettuce, and bruised tomatoes.

Chapter 26 – Undercover

As they drove to the police station, the cook talked incessantly about his large family; of those that had left Vieques to practice a Germanic language in strange lands. Feeling nostalgic, he wondered aloud what compelled them to emigrate. Family is everything, he said.

Although he was sitting right next to him, Demetrio wasn't listening. He anxiously rubbed his hands, clasped them together, and placed them over his mouth to exhale all his anxiety. His shame still lingered. He wanted to help Guillermo, but from afar, like the lighthouse keeper watching the storm in the distance. The uncertain fate of the two young lovers anguished him, as did his own. He realized, over and over, his failure as the adult in all of this, but did not know how to fix it. Amid all his thoughts, a shred of cowardice began to prevail. He was mortified by the thought of losing his license for violating the public drivers' ethics code.

How will I free myself from this nightmare, he wondered, scratching his head.

El Indio looked behind him at the boy in the cramped mobile kitchen. Guillermo's distraught visage made El Indio want to cry, but he refrained. Guillermo was lifeless, drained, as if he were dying. With all the knives and utensils surrounding him, the boy looked like a calf on its way to slaughter. It was then when El Indio finally heard the cook's words about how family provides support in times of need.

"Look, son! Where's your cell phone?" whispered Demetrio, regretting that he hadn't thought of it earlier.

Guillermo slowly pointed to the backpack.

"How come it isn't ringing? Has anyone called you? Your parents? Marisol's parents?"

"We turned them off, Don Demetrio. It was her idea."

"Shh! Don't mention my name. Wait until we get to the police station!"

Right at that moment, the truck halted, prompting everyone to lose their balance. The cook almost passed the entrance to the police station.

"Oh boy! I almost took you home with me. It wasn't until you said 'police station' that I remembered", he said chuckling. "I forgot. Since I was talking so much, Jeez!"

Demetrio gave him a side glance, thanked him for his help and helped Guillermo get out. The man wished them luck and left. Before entering the building, El Indio grabbed the boy by the shoulders and talked to him face to face.

"Look, I repeat, this is serious. Murphy's law says that whatever can go wrong, will go wrong. Back in Río Piedras I thought everything was going to be alright, but now, well, you see what can happen. Do me a favor and call your parents right now. Tell them that you're here and that you can't find your girlfriend. They will tell the authorities this important information. If your girlfriend was kidnapped, then it's a federal case. Hey, please, don't cry! Look at me. Think about this like a rite of passage, like changing from a boy to man, just like that! Another thing, don't call me Don Demetrio. Call me Indio. Demetrio doesn't exist, you understand? Call. Now!"

Guillermo turned on his phone and it went off like a techno cacophony of bells, sounds, and vibrations. He had hundreds of missed calls and dozens of text messages on his phone. The teenager called home. With sunken eyes, he heard his father yell from the other end of the line.

"I'm okay, Papi. Marisol is missing. I think she was kidnapped."

"Let me have it!" demanded Demetrio.

El Indio identified himself as a resident of Vieques. Without going into detail, he told the father to immediately call the authorities including the Coast Guard because they would be needing plenty of support. To avoid the tortuous desperate claims of the father, he passed the phone back to Guillermo and crossed the street.

"Papi, please tell Marisol's mother to forgive me." The boy hung up and ran after El Indio.

"Son, please forgive me, I'm not too smart. Crying is okay. When I was a boy if I cried, my grandmother would throw her sandal at me. And I'd stop crying very quickly," said Demetrio half-jokingly, pulling out his handkerchief to wipe the boy's face.

"Thanks, Indio. If it weren't for you, I don't know…"

"Don't worry. Marisol will appear, you'll see. Now get in there and start yelling like a madman. Tell them someone kidnapped Marisol. Describe the guy and say that someone told you he is called the Viking. Can you remember all that?"

"Yes, and you don't exist," said Guillermo, glancing at the building.

"Exactly. But look, I'll stay close by, and you know what? I'll call Ángel. Remember the guy who brought you here? He certainly knows a lot of people who can help us. C'mon, get do it!"

As soon as the boy entered the police station, Demetrio sent a text message to the fisherman: *9-1-1. Marisol is missing. Call. Urgent.*

Chapter 27 - A New Love

On his way home to La Hueca, El Cadi recalled how simple it had been to trap Marisol. He gloated over his skills. He rewound his thoughts back to the image of the kids under the palm trees. Upon seeing them kiss, his mind crossed the threshold from grey to a darker, more obscure place. He unzipped his pants to free his imprisoned penis. He stroked it and wet it with his own spit in forbidden satisfaction. Feeling like he was being watched by his mother, he was startled and squinted his eyes. He then imagined he was the one kissing Marisol. His sick pleasure floated over the image of the two bodies joined by a kiss. El Cadi smiled.

As soon as Marisol passed out and was left alone on the beach, El Cadi came out of his hideout to *rescue*—according to him—the perfect doll. "I've found you at last," he said repeatedly while picking her up and sniffing her neck. The broad chest of the so-called Viking enveloped Marisol's thin body. He went up the sliding sand dunes with ferocious determination. Once on the road, he saw lots of people on the sidewalk, so he slipped under the shadows of the dwarf palm trees, crouching like a lion hiding its prey. From a distance, he saw his car, the faithful witness to his crimes, and crossed the street. He looked both ways and waited for the right moment, that moment when everyone is focused on what they're doing, when they may be looking, but not seeing. He crossed the street and immediately opened his passenger-side door. From afar he saw Guillermo talking to the food truck cook. He placed Marisol inside and reclined the seat, carefully covering her with a folded beach towel. He looked left and right and closed the door. Before getting in himself, he wiped the disgusting sand from his skin.

Mommy, I found my little dolly. She'll be my favorite. She needs a new dress. She's mine and Ricky can't have her. What can I do to wipe that kiss off her lips? She'll only love me and kiss me sweetly. Those lips must be made of cotton candy. That's why he couldn't stop kissing her. I have to disinfect those lips and erase every trace of him. Perhaps with sandpaper. She's so pretty. Innocent. Mouthwatering. She's so beautiful, but her mouth is dirty. I'll use bleach...that's how I'll clean those lips. She's mine. I chose her. I'll dress her in short dresses. I'll buy her bows and shoes and bags and necklaces and watches and panties. She'll have everything she wants. She's so small. I'll comb her hair. French braids. I have to buy so many things. A tea set. What will I name her? Those lips; I have to clean those lips.

El Cadi reached La Hueca. He pulled out the remote controls and opened the first security gate, then the garage door. Once inside, he closed the two doors. He left the girl in the car. Before entering the house, he shook off the sand again. He went inside and washed his arms three times with plenty of soap. He ran to his bedroom and, from the top drawer of his bureau, he took out a manila envelope containing his documents and cash. He put it inside an old backpack. El Cadi returned to the drawer and pulled out the key to the basement. He took a deep breath before opening the door to the underground room.

"Thanks Mommy," he whispered, his nails scratching the ghostly eyes in the photo. He then went down the stairs.

"Asshole! I'm hungry," yelled Ricky. "I thought you were dead, but I see that today is not my lucky day."

El Cadi remained silent with his mind focused on only one thing. He repeated one word to himself: doll. He wanted to keep Ricky from reading his mind and discovering his new bliss. Looking up at the ceiling with nostalgia, he remembered his hundreds of still witnesses looking back at him, even through shut eyes.

They're crying for me. They sense that I'm leaving, he imagined.

The hundred or so dolls enshrouded in white looked like giant caterpillars suffering from not transforming into butterflies. With his back to Ricky, El Cadi wiped away a tear. He pushed the gurney closer to the cell. It was less than two feet away. He showed his brother the key and placed it on the fine white mattress.

"Call me the *Great Liberator* because today I will honor that name."

"What the hell is wrong with you? Did your mother's craziness finally burst?" yelled Ricky, snickering at his brother.

"Are you hungry? Let's have dinner together! That is, if you can reach the key."

El Cadi hurried out of the basement and grabbed the backpack in his room. He carefully peeked out the living room window. There was no one outside, as usual. For one last time, he opened all the doors binding him to his brother, pulled the car out of the garage and again closed all doors and gates. He smiled, relieved as he glanced at the house for the last time. He then turned to Marisol.

"How can I remove that stain from your mouth?" He moistened his fingers with his tongue and brusquely wiped the girl's lips.

With a satisfied smirk and a racing heart, he fled toward Sun Bay.

Chapter 28 - Amber Alert

The officers in the police station surrounded Guillermo when he entered screaming that his girlfriend had been taken.

"A man took her!", he yelled over and over.

The supervisor in charge of the shift was, at that moment, coming out of his office for a cup of coffee. He ordered the officer at the desk to take the boy to a room for questioning. Guillermo kneeled as he whimpered. Two officers pulled him up with the backpacks and escorted him to a room with a single table and two chairs. The boy knew that time was slipping and he immediately started talking about everything –Marisol and their plans for a romantic getaway, from the time they left Río Piedras, to the red-head, and the toxic juice.

"La Hueca, yes, the cook from the food truck told me that this man lives there. I saw him. I can identify him," said Guillermo, recognizing the name of the place while smacking his head.

One of the agents opened the door. He yelled to the officer at the front desk to send patrol cars to La Hueca. He then punched the keys on his phone to call his old friend from the Police Academy, now Captain of the police in Fajardo.

Immediately after, an AMBER Alert was sent throughout Puerto Rico and in Vieques. The radio and television channels aired emergency bulletins, and Marisol's friends and family uploaded photos of her on Instagram and Facebook. In a matter of minutes, thousands of followers from around the world pressed *Like*. And a local radio reporter broadcast the latest developments of the two missing teenagers.

In a special report, we are bringing you the latest information on the whereabouts of teenagers Guillermo Pérez López and Marisol Vargas Rosa, missing since this afternoon. According to reliable sources, the two are in the island municipality of Vieques. The boy, thirteen, is in the Vieques police station and is terrified by his schoolmate's disappearance. The authorities have not provided further information. This is all of the information we have at the moment. Reporting from your favorite radio station WAPA-Radio 680, Luis Ocasio, El Búho. The time: 10:38.

Chapter 29 - Playing the Role of a Man

As soon as Guillermo entered the police station, Demetrio hurried away, looking back several times. He went into a nameless grocery store down the block to buy a pack of cigarettes, and returned to the police station to see what was happening. The chiming of his cell phone interrupted his anxiety. It was Ángel. Demetrio told him everything and begged him to organize a search party with his friends. He asked if he knew of someone called the Viking in La Hueca.

"Yeah, they're a father and son, I remember them" said the fisherman. "Everyone knows everyone here. The one in La Hueca is the son because his father, Mr. Richard, lives above his business near the port. I always thought there was something off with his son. Do you understand? Where are you?"

"I'm in front of the police station. I left the boy in there by himself. You know, if he wanted to play grown up, well, today is his first day as a man."

"That's right! Okay Indio, I'll get my people together and stop by to pick you up."

"Thanks, brother."

The telephone at the police station sounded like a bell whose chime was possessed. After several calls, the officer in charge was able to confirm Guillermo's story. Meanwhile, the disturbing sound of a helicopter's spinning blades announced the confirmation of the search warrant signed by the judge. The large, metallic bird left San Juan, made a stop in Fajardo and then landed in Vieques. Authorities worked fast in response to the demands of the people of Puerto Rico. Everyone from the governor to the teens' classmates waited in anticipation of any new updates.

At once, the officer in charge dispatched with a number of agents and Guillermo to La Hueca. He sat in the back seat of the patrol car and was instructed to remain there at all times. They would be exercising caution every step of the way. The police knew nothing about the recluse El Cadi. As a matter of fact, he never gave any motive to be investigated for anything, even though the people in Vieques thought there was something suspicious about him.

As soon as they were given the order, two additional police vehicles joined the others in silently patrolling La Hueca. The silence in the area was unsettling. La Hueca boasted exclusive residences on spacious grounds. Even though most of the properties were well lit, it was still dark in the area, and visibility was limited. Many of these homes were surrounded by fences and looked like imprisoned mansions.

Ángel picked up Demetrio near the police station and followed the patrol cars joining the search. They followed at a cautious distance, even though the fisherman knew where El Cadi lived. Along the way, the official vehicles decorated the lush nocturnal forest with flickering blue lights until they landed in front of the house painted all white. The agents pulled out their weapons as they exited their vehicles. After crouching behind the open doors of their cars, one of the officers, with a loudspeaker in hand, ordered El Cadi to come out. Ángel parked on the side of the road before reaching the commotion. The rest of the fisherman's search party arrived at the same time. They stayed in their cars waiting for a signal. Behind them came more cars and more people on foot, mostly spectators.

☼

The phone rang in a business near the port of Isabel Segunda. Mr. Richard got up in the middle of the night, with aching bones. His mind was agile; his body was not. He thought the only person that might be calling at that hour of the night was Cadi. Holding onto the walls, he reached the desk in his office and lifted the handset. He answered familiarly, although he was annoyed, and then fell silent. He squeezed the handset and his mouth got dry when he heard an unfamiliar voice.

"The police are after your son," they said anonymously. Whoever it was hung up.

Dammit, Cadi! What have you done? But how many times have I told him… I don't know why I'm still here, since I knew he had no cure. If they didn't appreciate their mother, they certainly wouldn't appreciate me. Neither of them is worth the effort. Not even a great sacrifice will free them of their sins. They'll never change. Mr. Richard felt disappointed and miserable for having two twisted sons; he saw no future, no hope.

"When the police find the basement, they'll know everything," he said to himself. With the phone still in hand, he called someone he knew, and asked for a ride on a private boat to San Juan in Isla Grande. He planned to flee to Canada again. He hurried back to his room and dressed in sportswear. Despite the blinding rage, he was able to remember the right combination to his safe and gather his valuables. He went outside, let the dogs out, and closed the shop. As he waited on the street, he fidgeted with his keys to calm his nerves. He knew this moment was bound to come. He clenched the keys in his hands for a few seconds and dropped them in a storm sewer. He felt such selfish relief.

Chapter 30 - Free at Last

The commotion in La Hueca roused the neighbors. One by one the outdoor lights of each home turned on. Inside the homes, fleeting silhouettes cautiously slid the curtains for a peek. The more daring neighbors stepped outside barefoot and shirtless to witness the event. Couples inside their homes swore at those troublemakers disturbing such a peaceful night full of promising passion.

The officer with the loudspeaker, as if he were the leader of a revolution, continued threatening to break through the security walls if El Cadi refused to open.

In the basement, all Ricky thought about was being free. He looked around to see what he could use to help him reach the keys.

"Two feet, that's not too far," he uttered to himself. "Why now? I wonder what Cadi is up to. I don't know why I doubt him; we've been together in this house for so long. At last, he feels sorry for me. Dammit! Turn the volume down, freaky! Not only are you an idiot, you're deaf too! Come little keys, come to *daddy*," whispered Ricky.

With a rolled up t-shirt he tried reaching one of the gurney's wheels. He craved food and pleasures, and all he needed was to be free to enjoy them. The t-shirt was too thin to move the wheel; he needed something thicker. He took off his sweatpants, ripped them at the crotch, wet them, and twirled them until they were as thick as a rope. His sweatpants were the first step towards freedom. Although he was cold-blooded by nature, his hands trembled when he finally placed the key in the old lock. At last, the metal bars opened for him.

"Oh happy day!" he sang as he walked partially naked up the stairs.

He was still trembling when he opened the door to the house and glanced at Dolly's picture. He looked at it for a while and then spit on it. Once inside, the noise he was hearing got louder. He thought Cadi might be enjoying an action movie and stopped to take a good look at his brother's room. It was simple, clean, white: it was immaculate. He entered his brother's bathroom. Everything was impeccable: white curtains and rug. In a fit, he lowered the toilet lid and peed on it. He also peed on the floor and in the tub. He spat in the sink. Had he the need to defecate, he would have, but he had last eaten twelve hours ago. He felt so much bottled-up talent in expressing his wickedness. But now that he was free, he remained paralyzed when he saw his face in the bathroom mirror. He approached it. He had a long, red, scruffy beard that draped his nearly transparent skin. His dark eyes stood out from beneath his long, red tangled locks.

I need to be loved, he thought while combing his beard. Without wasting any more time, he went to get something to eat in the kitchen. He thought he would find his brother in the dining room. He remained curious about his surroundings and looked everywhere. It was his first time seeing the house. He smiled at Cadi's bad taste. *Why is everything so white*, he wondered. He was more and more overwhelmed and what he thought was noise from the television drove him crazy.

There was no one in the kitchen. He opened the refrigerator, grabbed a beer and drank it in three long gulps. The racket was becoming unbearable. He opened another beer and sensed the particular cold liquid going down to his empty stomach. Out of the haze, he finally heard someone repeating out loud: *We have you surrounded. Come out now or we'll break the door in.*

"Hey, a*sshole*, are you deaf?" yelled Ricky looking up at the ceiling, unable to determine where to direct his voice.

After belching, he turned to the refrigerator again and pulled out a container. He opened it. Inside was raw meat. He took a big bite out of the meat and swallowed it almost without chewing. He was about to take a second bite when a bang shook the foundation of the house. The electricity when out for a few seconds. Outside, the police crane knocked down the front gate. Like a lost ant, Ricky attempted to find his way out. During the few seconds of darkness, he noticed the blinking lights outside. He now understood that his brother had set him up.

"Damn you, Cadi!"

As his shoulder pushed open the kitchen door leading to the garage, another impact shook the house. The lights blinded him. Confused, he covered his eyes with one arm, and lifted his other arm with the piece of meat in his hand. Gripping the meat firmly, dozens of red drops ran down his arm.

Two armed officers that entered the garage during the second shock pushed him to the ground, and another two entered the house.

"They got him!" yelled the people outside.

Guillermo watched everything from the police car. He was asked to identify the kidnapper. The partially naked man looked familiar, but not quite.

It's not possible for him to have grown a beard and all that hair in a few hours. This isn't the guy, he thought in frustration.

"Marisol!" cried Guillermo as he sprinted toward the house.

"Wait, you can't go in!" Guillermo was warned.

As the officers handcuffed Ricky, Guillermo shouted that he was not the man who kidnapped his girlfriend.

"What do you mean this isn't the guy?" asked the officer in charge, grabbing the boy by the arm.

"It's not him. It looks like him, but this one has a long beard. The other guy doesn't," said Guillermo, sobbing again.

"Don't worry! My men are inspecting the house."

After several very long minutes, a voice interrupted the officer in charge:

"Boss, there's no one else inside, but we found something interesting."

"What?"

"A basement with a cage! We have to send over a team to investigate."

Guillermo knelt and dropped his head in his arms. The officer in charge ordered the agents to seal the doors with yellow tape and stay guarding the property, while waiting for the detectives to arrive. Two other officers escorted the boy to the car. He wept with his head hanging, when he heard someone softly call his name. He was able to make out El Indio and Ángel. He shook his head and mouthed to them: "Find Marisol."

Demetrio and Ángel nodded.

Wasting no time, the fisherman pulled out his cell phone and wrote: *She's still missing. Let's separate into groups. Each group search your neighborhood. Now!*

As they left La Hueca, Ángel and El Indio talked about the man in handcuffs. Ángel lamented the unprecedented tragedy that was unfolding here.

"I have never in my life seen that scruffy lowlife. I even bet that no one even knew he existed. I don't like this. There's something fishy here!" said Ángel.

"Oh, man, I feel so guilty," said El Indio.

"Forget about it. We have to focus on finding that girl."

Chapter 31 - Sun Bay

El Cadi drove cautiously, but freely due south toward Sun Bay. Once there, he would come up with a plan to escape to the nearby island of Culebra. His breathing was agitated as he thought about how he would have to row out to the open sea. He was afraid of the sea. In his mind, he envisioned himself with Marisol on a small boat on their way to a place where he could enjoy her small body. He was already hyperventilating and had to stop the car on the side of the road in order to calm his racing heart. With his hands on the wheel, he thought about his brother being locked up again and laughed like a hysterical child.

On Flamboyán Street, near the businesses in Esperanza, he slowed down to avoid attracting attention. Even though the night was getting late, the area still bustled with activity. Young people and adults all went in and out of bars, prolonging the night. El Cadi managed to drive his vehicle—like a phantom—through the town without catching anybody's eye.

El Cadi entered the beach at Sun Bay through a hidden entrance that only the people of Vieques knew about. He drove to the visitors' parking lot, with its white lines erased by the sand. He noticed several vehicles parked at a distance from one another. They erotically rocked side-to-side, like boats adrift in a tropical storm. Knowing that he was invisible to them, he immediately drove to the farthest end of the parking, through one of the narrow paths covered by thorny brush. Suddenly, he let out a cry and slammed his car's horn when two herons, startled by the car's bright lights, suddenly flew out of the mangrove trees. He nervously pushed the gas pedal, and the harder he pushed, the more the car slid into the mud. But El Cadi pushed on, relentlessly, brusquely. Sweating and obsessed, he was determined to cross to the other side.

The couples hiding in the other cars abandoned their moment of pleasure in hearing the racket. In unison, they cursed the bold disturbance of romance. They lifted their heads, uneasy. Once more, El Cadi pushed the pedal and fled through the path toward his hiding place between the mangroves. When he felt safe enough, he stopped the car and turned off the lights. He left Marisol on the seat, wrapped in a towel to protect her from the mosquitos. She was still asleep. The effect of the drug would remain for many more hours in her thin body. He, excited over the innocence he would soon shatter, brushed his huge fingers against her lips. Wasting no time, he pulled out a flashlight from the glove compartment and closed the door, leaving Marisol inside. He locked the car and shone the light on the ground to avoid stepping in puddles of mud. Step by step, he found his way out and attempted to find a safe route to carry his doll. He knew where to go. After years of spying on people in Vieques, he knew many of their secrets. That was how he found out about the fishing boats hiding inside the growing brush along the public beach. They tied the boats to tree stumps and took tourists on boat rides when not fishing. They called themselves the Sombé tour guides, and this way they earned extra cash to take home to their families.

El Cadi searched the boats to find one in the best condition possible. Being adrift after such a perfect plan would be stupid, he thought. He found one in excellent condition, although it was missing its oars. He continued along the muddy path until he saw a white boat ahead, far from the others. He crossed the narrow and briny way, often shaking his boots and swore with each step, disgusted by the mud caked on his boots. This boat had oars. He untied it and dragged it to the shoreline.

El Cadi abruptly stopped. He thought he heard sounds like the ones in the action movies he enjoyed. They were harsh sounds mixed together: the crashing waves, a boat motor at high speed, and helicopter blades. He turned off his flashlight, crouched next to the boat and listened carefully.

They must be tourists, because the police are surely quite busy with Ricky, he thought. He then went into the brush to fetch Marisol.

Chapter 32 – Esperanza

The night was advancing. No text messages, either with good news or bad, appeared on Ángel's cell phone. He and Demetrio set out to find Marisol. They went from Mosquito Bay to Sun Bay—or Sombé, which is how the people of Vieques pronounced it. The moon was full, therefore, the tiny bioluminescent creatures in Sun Bay were hidden. Out and about, however, were visible swarms of mosquitos that clung to any warm-blooded body passing by. Ángel was used to the mosquitos, but Demetrio felt them bite, as if his grandmother's bee had been multiplied by a hundred.

The police went from house to house in La Hueca to see if someone, anyone, had heard of something unusual happening in the Viking's residence. Meanwhile, another group of officers patrolled the businesses in Esperanza where El Cadi was last seen.

Without involving the authorities, the fishermen decided to mobilize and surround the Vieques coast. Even if they did not know the victim, they faithfully followed Ángel's instructions. He was their leader. They divided into groups of two and covered the island from west—Punta Arenas—to east, an area restricted by the U.S. Navy. The fisherman's honest involvement was appreciated more by the people of Vieques, who were often put on the back burner by politicians promising to help the island.

Dozens of young and curious residents gathered and followed the police on foot to find out details about the girl keeping everyone on alert. The crowds of onlookers were misinterpreted by the tourists walking through Esperanza. They thought the locals were always partying, bunching together here and there to simply celebrate life on the beach.

There were youngsters everywhere. The more daring of them even knew how to trespass Puerto Diablo—restricted by the Navy—without getting noticed, or so they believed, on the federal radars.

Before entering Sombé, the fisherman and El Indio searched Playa Grande and Playa Negra, without noticing anything suspicious. The only melody interrupting the solitude was the blend of boisterous waves that insisted on crashing against the coastal cays and coral reefs. As they searched the area, Ángel interrupted the increasingly disheartening silence.

"I'm going to tell you something that not even the police may suspect," said the fisherman. "We here in Vieques believe that our women go missing because they want to."

"What do you mean?"

"They admit amongst themselves how miserable they are here. We've heard them. And the worst part is that they are right. What do we have to offer to them? There's not even good fishing here. We're bombarded by a neglect that hurts, brother, in every aspect."

"But Marisol's case is different and you know it," said Demetrio, scratching his mosquito bites.

"Why do you think we've mobilized this way? That girl isn't from these parts, you see. And if we don't act fast, our little island will be filled with nosy onlookers. The pig who ran off with her deserves to be lynched. Really! I don't understand how we didn't notice there were two of them!"

"Which explains a lot. Don't you think?"

"Look, Mr. Richard was always at his business and we don't mess much with foreigners, because they bring money, tourists, and they work. Do you understand? And his other son, I guess, remained invisible until today. The owner of the Blue Moon is the only one who has had the most contact with him. I once heard him say that the Viking was a weird guy, who visited his business at the same hour every evening. He is the quiet type, preferring to keep to himself. You see?"

"And he tricked everyone."

"Right. I hope there aren't any more hidden redheads, otherwise I'll think they're cloning Viking pirates here."

"Those guys have to be on the run or something. But why? I'm sorry brother, but after finding out about these odd characters, I suspect Vieques will be flooded with bad news for a while."

"Yep, until the media focuses its attention on Cuba again."

"That's life, *chiquitico,*" said Demetrio, imitating a Cuban accent.

Ángel chuckled and said nothing else.

Chapter 33 - The Feds Arrive

After midnight, two Coast Guard boats patrolled the entire Vieques coastline at high speed. Their two beams lit the beach and the sea like dragon fire. Hovering above was a duo of helicopters from the main island of Puerto Rico, sometimes maneuvering impromptu landings on areas near the port of Isabel Segunda. One had reporters and their camera crew, the other brought a group of men dressed in jackets and jeans. By their sunglasses and haircuts, everyone knew they were Feds. Meanwhile, a group of volunteer policemen from Fajardo reinforced the search on private boats.

Back at the police station, Guillermo's body was warming the witness seat in the commander's office. He had no choice but to tell the truth if he wanted to help Marisol. His pale, exhausted face was etched in misery and suffering. Had he shed tears of blood, his face would have been completely red. His sole desire was to see Marisol. He was alone and his chest hurt. His breathing was shallow and he thought he was going to die, but he begged God for one more day to be with his girlfriend alive and well again. He bent his legs, propped them up on the edge of his seat, and folded his arms over his aching chest to protect it. Rolled into a ball, with his head between his knees, he blamed himself for everything. He regretted ignoring his gut instincts. Since his parents had not yet arrived and although he now had the chance to become a man and speak his testimony, he couldn't without his parents' consent. The authorities ironically, had to wait in these kidnapping cases because of laws protecting minors. His parents' signature on his written testimony is only a bureaucratic afterthought, but the authorities couldn't continue searching for Marisol without it.

Chapter 34 - Help at Sombé

When El Indio and the fisherman arrived at the Sun Bay parking lot, they honked the car's horn three times to warn the couples having clandestine encounters to take a break. The rocking movement of the cars was less intense now. Some of the couples lifted their heads curiously, like sea turtles. Others swore and some pulled out their middle fingers. Two interruptions in a single night was too much. Ángel cautiously approached the first parked vehicle.

"Excuse me, have you seen anything suspicious in the past half hour?"

"Like what?" said a man whose nude torso hid someone else's.

"I don't know! Like someone running away?"

"We're all on the run." The couple snickered. "Ask someone else, you jerk!"

Before approaching another vehicle, the already disheartened Ángel turned on his blinking emergency lights. His car looked like a lost firefly in the woods. He was ashamed to interrupt the intimate encounters. He asked the same question to each vehicle, and they answered that the only weird thing they had seen was a Jeep burning rubber as it penetrated the coastal brush at the western part of the parking lot. The fisherman hurried and parked near that area. Both he and El Indio got out of the car. With their cell phones' flashlights, they were able to see the fresh tire tracks. Before entering the maze of coastal trees, Ángel sent a text message to the other fishermen: *We need help in Sombé.*

Demetrio and Ángel exchanged glances, even in the darkness, and bumped fists in a show of camaraderie. Guided by the fresh tire tracks, they followed the path of the flattened bushes formed by El Cadi's car. In the serpentine way filled with obstacles, they found trash left behind by campers, as well as thousands of mosquito larvae reproducing themselves in stagnant pools of water. Shining their flashlights everywhere, they zigzagged their way through, careful to avoid a fall that might impede their search. Silently, the two friends penetrated the swamp's humid core. The disarray in that minuscule space of the Caribbean contained a sinister atmosphere inviting evil, perhaps inviting a violent attack. Even though the two men themselves were peaceful, at that moment they felt an irrational hatred toward anyone with the heinous desire to ravage the girl. If they found him, they would gouge his eyes out, tear his skin off, burn him alive, and then bury whatever was left of him deep in the ancient earth, almost touching hell.

The fisherman suddenly lifted his arm. They stopped. Not even ten paces away was El Cadi's car. The two approached it holding their breath, fearing they would see Marisol inside, naked and stiff with her eyes open like a fish. The car was empty. With their chests stirring from the rush of adrenaline, they cautiously continued their way on dry land until they found several boats. They examined them and found nothing. They made their way lightly to the beach. The fisherman thought he heard some mumbling sounds coming from the sea grape bushes. He turned right on the next curve along the path covered in wet leaves, and found an empty boat. Instinctively, they followed the sound of the waves embracing the shoreline. Before reaching the opening to the sea, they saw a large shadow and a confusing flash of light. They immediately covered their cell phone flashlights. Demetrio, suddenly feeling a momentary wave of rage overshadow his reasoning, almost darted over to the unknown figure, but Ángel stopped him. El Indio looked like he was spewing smoke through his nose and mouth. He lifted both his arms, however, showing Ángel that he was in control.

El Cadi stood by the boat carrying something in his arms. It was Marisol. With utmost care, he placed the girl in the small boat and caressed her hair, whispering tender words to her, like a father to his newborn daughter.

His carnal desires softened, and he promised to end his stalking in order to keep his sole prey: Marisol. With an idiotic expression, he dreamed he would tame her, shape her at will, like a clay figure. He would force her to worship him like an almighty god. He smiled, immersed in his perverse thoughts, and imagined having a life with her somewhere else, and even with a family. This was a new and perfect opportunity to erase the nightmares of his past. He would change his name, as his father had done. He would attempt, albeit with difficulty, to tear Ricky out of his soul. It was Ricky's fault El Cadi suffered panic attacks every time his mother's death came to mind. Nonetheless, he enjoyed sharing his first murder with his brother; it was an accomplishment that triggered the beginning of an unwittingly inherited madness. In any case, El Cadi could now enjoy a freedom from his family, freedom to become the hero like in his favorite films. As he wondered what film Marisol could be in, he heard the crunching sound of dry leaves coming from the bushes. He slowly got up, praying it was an egret.

Behind, the two rescuers kept still. Ángel looked everywhere hoping that at least one of his search groups was close by, but the only thing moving closer to them were the waves. Within seconds, the clouds covering the moon drifted west. It was then that the fisherman was able to clearly see El Cadi, and told El Indio that he was indeed the Viking's son.

"That's one big son of a bitch," whispered Demetrio.

He turned to his friend to start the countdown and immediately Ángel counted to three. Their shouting was like the war cries from their Taíno ancestors. They charged forward lifting small clouds of sand along the way. El Cadi watched everything unfold in disbelief, his body remained still while his thoughts flew by, flashing with death, sobs, jail, sex, dolls, and loneliness. He was motionless, like a ship's figurehead. He was stunned by the two strangers rushing towards him. He fell to his knees and covered his head with his arms. The two warriors started striking blows, hitting him multiple times on the temples, his back, and his stomach. The Viking was confused, yet it seemed as if the hard horned helmet of his ancestors was protecting him. El Cadi stumbled with each haphazard blow. However, with a crazed look on his face, the twin brother grabbed the two by their shirts and lifted them ten inches off the ground. He then let out a loud and resounding cry, mustering enough unharnessed strength to drop one on top of the other.

El Cadi saw the seconds vanish as his scheme was thwarted. That attack did not figure into his plans of a new life with Marisol; instead it had punctured a hole in them, emptying them out. He tried to run, but his feet slipped on the sand and he fell on all fours. The thought of him covered in sand, beaten by a pair of old idiots without weapons invigorated him. Sweat dripped down his forehead into his spiteful eyes. He saw that one of his attackers laid unconscious from the fall, and saw the other one, rising slowly in confusion. It was then El Cadi shot up. He grabbed one of the boat's oars and ran unbridled toward him. He knocked him down on the sand again with a blow to his shoulder, and with the tip of the oar he whacked him on the forehead and tore his skin. Blinded by fury, the twin sat on him and grabbed him by the hair. The fisherman's head looked small in El Cadi's barbaric hands. Thinking about his thwarted escape, he hit Ángel's head repeatedly against the packed sand. The constant sound of his head hitting the ground was like that of a burial drum. El Cadi picked up the fisherman's limp body like a rag doll, wacked it, and dragged it to the water and it sunk at will.

Ángel's soul left his body after the second blow with the oar, but in his fury El Cadi kept kicking it. Unable to fully understand what had just happened, the Viking yelled furiously at the wind. In that uncontrollable state, he even thought that the man would come back to life at any moment, like a zombie from one of his many violent video games. He then heard voices. The rest of the fishermen summoned by Ángel had arrived. When they saw El Cadi savagely beating their leader's limp body, they all grabbed stones, sticks, whatever they could, and ran angrily toward him. Frightened by the crowd, El Cadi sped back to the boat. He realized he couldn't escape with Marisol. He looked at her, still placidly asleep, and punched the bow so hard that it cracked.

"I swear by the devil himself, I'll find you!" he said in a trembling voice. Swiftly grabbing his backpack, he pulled out a knife and placed it between his teeth.

Demetrio, dazed by the fall, could not get up as quickly as he wanted. His stiff bones were still quivering. Confused, he turned to his side and, although his vision remained hazy, his eyes were still able to follow the sinister reflection of a floating ball going deeper into the sea. Another one of the fishermen helped him up. Sitting on the wet sand, he closed and opened his eyes several times, attempting to adjust his focus on the ebb and flow of the waves. Still confused, he thought his mind was playing tricks on him. He gently leaned against the fisherman and pointed to the beach so that he would see for himself the single buoy slowly making its way out to sea.

"If that's the Viking, he won't get very far. The others are going after him," said the fisherman in convincing certainty.

Chapter 35 – Digitalized

The police joined the federal authorities to thoroughly piece together the secrets behind the three Richards, who had been living in Vieques for over a decade. Upon scanning a recent photo of Mr. Richard found in his desk, the criminal records of about a hundred similar men appeared on the screen. The U.S. security network was very accurate, and given that Mr. Richard's appearance had changed very little, the agents matched him with his profile. He appeared under another last name. In bright red letters, he was described as missing and wanted by the U.S. authorities. His profile also indicated that he was a suspect in his wife's death in Michigan, and in the disappearance of his sons.

After the AMBER Alert earlier in the night, all the local and international sea ports and airports were provided with a photo of Marisol. Pictures of her were also posted on social media and highway banners. Apart from the authorities, many night owls followed the case on their cell phones, tablets, and computers in real time. In fact, they received minute-by-minute alerts about the capture in Vieques, and the alleged kidnapper and fugitive, a foreign man also known as the Viking.

Some people in Vieques took photos of Ricky's arrest. The image inevitably rippled through the cyber ocean. What astonished people the most was how he looked with his cheeks covered in blood, partially naked, and dirty. On their devices they pored over the enlarged image of the man to see every part of his body in detail: his reddish hair tangled and disheveled, his squinting eyes blinded by the powerful lights, his chest covered in dark hair spattered in the blood from the raw meat he squeezed in his left hand. He looked like a caveman. *What kind of monster is that?* wondered people.

Journalists missed their chance to snap that picture and suffered the most. It would have been worth thousands of dollars. The public beat them to the punch. The city's editors squirmed in frustration upon seeing the pictures all over social media and would not stop calling their employees to see who was available immediately to find out more about the savage in captivity. After these photos, even the story of Marisol's disappearance was pushed to the back burner.

The police station in Vieques also added Ricky's picture to their data base. All three—the father and his sons—looked so much alike, that it was hard to miss their relation. It would be easier now to identify the missing puzzle pieces: Mr. Richard and El Cadi. Although little was known about El Cadi in Vieques, the arrest of his twin brother roused things. In addition, the discovery of the weird basement in the house prompted the federal authorities in Puerto Rico to come running. Some of them expected to find something macabre in that basement, with the hopes of advancing their careers. They thought of the worst when they heard about the hundreds of maimed dolls hanging from the basement ceiling. *What heinous acts were committed here?* they thought. In their detective minds, they thought they would surely find buried victims.

"Only God knows what diabolical rituals these loons held here," said one of the detectives while snapping photos of the room.

"This ceremony must surely be created by these savages," added another federal agent, placing small jars containing tiny fingernails into a plastic evidence bag.

Chapter 36 – Seahorses

El Cadi managed to escape by swimming away. He was heading toward Culebra. He reached a buoy near the beach and with his knife, cut the cord connecting the floating balls. From the corner of the triangle linked by the three brother towns, Vieques, Culebra, and Fajardo, he could see their blinking lights. But he was also alone within the world's darkness. Everything was murky. With his gaze lost, he held on tight to the buoy and kicked non-stop because he knew they were after him. Fear got the best of him and made him lose his focus, sinking deeper into his thoughts. His wet clothes and shoes made believe he was inevitably sinking, as he struggled to keep his head afloat with his huge, now tired arms. The Viking was hallucinating. He believed the waves had acquired a life of their own and were intent on drowning him. Swallowing so much salt water made it difficult for him to breathe.

Not far behind, eight expert swimmers were catching up. Distressed, El Cadi changed the way he moved his legs to keep them from cramping, but he was getting tired. He tried to keep moving, but his hiking boots hampered his progress. He tried removing them, but he panicked when he swallowed more water. His throat burned. He vomited. He was exhausted. Without much choice, he relaxed his body and tried not to drown. As if he were in another time and dimension, he was stunned by the peacefulness of the full moon. Its pale roundness comforted him. He let himself float along the silent current then closed his eyes, as if attempting to hide from himself, and two tears fell from his eyes into the sea. He wanted to preserve his strength for the upcoming attack. And then, he dropped his backpack and turned faced down to contemplate the immensity of the ocean rocking him. Perhaps if he played dead they would let him go, he thought. He took a deep breath and let himself sink. Deep. The impossible return. This was how he would fool them. From under the water he could make out the moon up above and felt his heart throb in his throat. Eight seconds later, he was pulled out and beaten by what he believed were a dozen sea monsters and their giant tentacles. He then exhaled the remaining air in his lungs and thrashing about, attempted to break free from the beast of the sea torturing him. A fleeting thought came to mind: *Dolly is calling me.*

One of the men had a harpoon and was waiting for the right moment to pierce El Cadi's body. Two men held him by the arms, and others pulled his legs into the darker, colder current. El Cadi was captured by the fishermen, men who called themselves seahorses; preferring, generation after generation, the sea over land.

The Viking pushed and pulled, tried breaking free with the last sharp movements he had left, but the lack of air hampered his desire to live. Now, hopelessly weak, El Cadi surrendered to the struggle. Without even a slither of strength, he opened his mouth and let out one last choked cry. Finally, releasing their rage through what they thought as a fair punishment, the fisherman with the harpoon shot El Cadi below the left nipple and immediately a braided string of blood painted the water a purplish hue. Two other fishermen jumped in to hold his legs, while the other two went up to get some air. They traded off this time tying El Cadi's cold body with the buoy's rope to a mine underwater marked with a cross. It was supposedly inactive.

Chapter 37 – Omen

Mr. Richard, meanwhile, was escaping with absolutely no problem at all, going from the Marina del Rey port in Fajardo to the airport in Isla Verde. He drove himself in the car he kept at Marina del Rey for when he ran errands in San Juan.

When he reached the airport and was getting out of the car, his legs were trembling so badly he had to remain sitting for a few minutes until he calmed down. He then got out of the car, walked around to the trunk and pulled out his bag. His palms were sweating and he let go of his bag to wipe them with a handkerchief from his pants pocket. When he closed the back door, he saw a hazy image in the glass and panicked. It was his own reflection. He wacked it with his hand and catching his breath, leaned against the car.

His breathing was shallow. He looked everywhere. There was no one in the parking lot.

My paranoia is killing me, he thought.

The day was already breaking, but it was still dark. Nonetheless, he pulled out darken glasses—one of many El Cadi threw away—from his bag's outer pocket and put them on. He then started walking somewhat at ease.

I'm too old for this, he thought, pushing back the sunglasses that slid down his nose. He left the parking area through the pedestrian walkway connecting the airport's four terminals. In the distance he could hear the echo of a conversation between two luggage carriers waiting by one of the exits. The lights were still off in the food stands and the airline counters.

A passenger or two, either coming or going, would pass by dragging luggage, and the rhythmic clicking of their wheels against the floor irritated Mr. Richard's nerves more and more.

Since he had his boarding pass on his cell phone, he was able to breeze through the security checkpoint. He felt envy from the other passengers waiting in the line where both bodies and luggage are inspected. After passing each station on his way through the airport, he sighed in relief. Once inside the terminal he stopped sweating, and his breathing returned to normal. But the federal authorities were tracking him the whole time. One of the agents on duty in the airport spotted him on a terminal's hidden cameras.

He kept a frightened gaze behind his shades when they saw him entering Terminal D. For three full hours, the Feds allowed him to relax. He crossed his legs, first one way then the other, while leafing through a sports car magazine.

On the very first boarding call, Mr. Richard sprang up spryly to board the plane bound north. But just as he was handing his ticket to freedom to the airline employee, two undercover federal agents came out from behind a door that, until then, no one had noticed. As Mr. Richard extended his arm to the employee, one of the Feds slapped handcuffs on his wrists and the other read him his rights in both English and Spanish. Everything happened so quickly that most of the people waiting by the exit gate did not even notice. Without resisting arrest, Mr. Richard sighed in frustration. Now, devoid of all hope, he looked up at the ceiling, as if expecting Dolly to rescue him from the hell awaiting him on Earth.

Chapter 38 – Contrast

Even Ricky did not understand why he had been arrested. He was completely free for about only five minutes when suddenly, amid all the racket coming from what he thought was an action movie, he was trapped in a police hunt without even knowing why. The confusion overtook him, and he simply followed without resisting. He merely observed in order to make sense of his new imprisonment.

Ricky always thought he was smarter than his brother, but this time he had to hand it to El Cadi. He now had little use for the mental control he always had over his brother. He was definitely surprised, however, by this move against him. To flee and have someone else take the blame was sheer genius. When they were children, he was the one who planned schemes against his brother. This time, however, the tables had turned. The apprentice outdid the master, thought Ricky, cursing his twin's accomplishment.

A sharp pain hammered Ricky's chest while seated in the patrol car bound for the police station in Vieques.

I hope I die, he thought attempting to connect with his brother through telepathy. *How dare he leave me alone in this damned place! I know nothing here! Now he's done it, now he's gone crazy. And my good-for-nothing father is nowhere to be found. I don't understand what's going on.*

The only recollection Ricky had of Vieques was the day he arrived at the age of fourteen. At that moment in time, he wasn't even interested in observing the surrounding island landscape. Now, at last, with chains and locks up and down his body, he was stunned by the contrasting blues and greens of the sea and the mountains. He was able to appreciate them, only briefly, through the triangular window of the armored police car.

Ricky decided to remain silent until he understood what the investigation was about. If his father abandoned him again, he would need a lawyer. He knew his rights very well, he learned about them on the television programs he saw each day. He was certain that when El Cadi showed up everything would be clarified in Ricky's favor. He then smiled self-assuredly, just as he had when he saw Dolly exhale for the last time.

That very same morning, Ricky was transferred to a federal prison in Puerto Rico. He would have to wait there until the confusion over his identity was clarified. He knew very well that his last name entailed a burden over his fateful past, and it now led to an uncertain future.

Walking in short paces with the shackles, he wished he were Houdini in one of his escape acts. When the steel doors opened, he was sorry to have left behind the key to his cell in La Hueca. He cursed again upon seeing his nearly transparent and dirty skin under the light of the day.

Cadi, my little brother, please help me get out of here, he thought in anguish. Outwardly, though, he displayed self-imposed calmness.

Chapter 39 – Sacrifice

The fishermen picked up Ángel's body and placed it on the sand next to the boat where Marisol lay. The respect they had for that man was so great, they treated him as if he were asleep.

In the distance, a police siren was wailing and nearing. The onlookers who arrived before the police ran like hermit crabs to the boat to shine their cell phone flashlights on the sleeping beauty. Everyone wanted to photograph her first to show their crude image to the world, regardless of whether she was dead or alive.

Demetrio, still sitting on the sand, saw everything as if in a haze, but then brushed his ear after hearing a restless bee buzzing. The thought of finding out that Marisol had died horrified him. Annoyed by the crowd of prying youngsters, he caught a second wind and got up effortlessly. He pushed his way through the crowd and to the boat, attempting to see Marisol. Instead he found Ángel's body on the ground surrounded by the fishermen. His friend's bloodied face compelled him to kneel over his body and weep at his feet.

"No, Ángel, no! *Ay, bendito!* Why you? You're the last person who should be here!" he said, sobbing.

One of the fishermen tapped him lightly on the shoulder.

"He's been avenged," said the partially dressed man with a harpoon in his hand, who then scurried into the thick brush when the police and paramedics arrived.

"Do you know if the girl…?" asked Demetrio, with hopelessness in his voice.

No one answered. The fishermen understood that the most important thing at that moment was to pay respects to their leader. El Indio, respectful, but also concerned about Marisol, went over to the boat. He drove out the onlookers and peeked into the slanted vessel. The girl was unharmed, just like when he picked her up in the Río Piedras terminal the day before. Her lips were swollen; her face was serene. Trembling, Demetrio brushed aside the hair hiding her cheeks. He got closer to sense whether she was breathing or whether he was about to suffer another loss.

"She's breathing!" yelled Demetrio.

The crowd cheered and photo flashes from their cell phones went off. Demetrio was annoyed at such rudeness, but he was also so tired and brokenhearted that he had no strength left to fight. He silently thanked the divine spirit for letting Marisol live. He was happy because she would keep the memory of her first kiss there in Vieques, the way she wanted. But Demetrio went from romantic analysis to absurd questioning:

Would this tender child be able to live in peace after realizing the tragedy her whims have caused? Two men have just died for her. The things that come to my head! Oh, what does it matter? I think I'm going crazy. I guess I should go on with my life. And please God, keep me away from ever giving a ride to people in love again!

Before anyone and without permission, Demetrio lifted Marisol up from the boat. He contemplated her, even asleep. The girl looked like an angel, harmless.

"My child, what mischief! I hope you and Guillermo have learned that falling in love is a complicated matter," he whispered. And then he gave her a fatherly kiss on the forehead.

Seconds later, authorities came to the rescue. They arrived through the beach, which was the safest way. The fishermen stayed put around Ángel's body to keep anyone from taking pictures. The rest of the crowd surrounded Demetrio, who was leaning against the boat with Marisol in his arms.

A photo of Demetrio with the girl traveled in real time through social media. That was how Marisol's and Guillermo's parents, their classmates, and even people on the other side of the planet found out about what had happened.

She's alive in her hero's arms, was the headline accompanying the photo. Also reading the story were Demetrio's two children and his string of ex-girlfriends, all wondering what the hell he was doing in Vieques as the main character of that event.

The police officers shone powerful flashlights on people's faces, asking them about the suspect, while El Indio placed Marisol on the ambulance gurney. He feared getting entangled too deeply in the case. Saving him from federal probing, however, was the constant activity of the crowd. With so many people on the beach, federal authorities had a hard time making a clear investigation.

At daybreak, the crowd started dispersing along the different paths leading out of Sombé. At last, all the commotion of the previous night was coming to an end, and the people of Vieques would be able to rest. Some of the fishermen decided to take advantage of the placid waves to venture out into the open water and try to find a good catch. Two fishermen volunteered to carry Ángel's body.

♥

The authorities believed El Cadi was a fugitive. The residents and fishermen they interviewed all said they had seen him swim out to sea on a buoy. He escaped, said most of the people. A drawing of El Cadi was sent around through the news media. All of the Caribbean islands were alerted and provided with his profile and his mugshot, only it was actually his brother Ricky's face without the beard and long hair. Security measures increased in Puerto Rico, as a result. Any tall man with reddish hair and freckled skin was observed with caution. The internet was on alert and new group chats were started where people commented about seeing him in Culebra and even several of the other Lesser Antilles. Others surmised that perhaps he was at the bottom of the sea or hidden away aboard a yacht belonging to a foreign tycoon. Only the discovery of his body, either dead or alive, would comfort the people's thoughts.

Chapter 40 - And Life Goes On After Every Sunset

El Indio carefully broke away from the crowd and sat facing the sea on a petrified tree trunk. He pulled out his cell phone from his pocket and swore when he saw the screen was shattered.

Son of a bitch Viking!

He then realized it was on, despite being wet. It only had one percent of power left. He considered telling Guillermo about everything that happened, and that Marisol was alive, although he was sure the boy already knew all about it. So, before his device reached techno limbo, he wrote him a text message. Just as he pressed the *send* button, the phone died.

"Another one bites the dust," he said in anger, throwing the phone into the sea.

Demetrio had been awake for the past twenty-four hours, without dinner and only nicotine flowing through his body. Exhausted, he fell face-up on the sand and cried. It was the same sadness as the day when they told him his grandmother had died. He sobbed inconsolably with a dull sensation in his chest. He was barely able to breath and remained with his mouth agape, searching for air like a fish. Suddenly, he felt something jump on his nose.

"Dammit! What is that?"

He got up startled by an insect that almost entered his open mouth. It was a horsefly.

Is that abuela in disguise? he wondered, recalling how much he loved his grandmother.

Despite the pain he was in and the sorrow over having lost his friend, he knew then and there that life would go on with or without him. He would honor Ángel, as he had his grandmother and his predecessors. Despite having lived an unprecedented day, full of sadness and alarming situations, life would, indeed, go on after every sunset.

From the past, I'll only remember what will help me in the future, he thought, calmer now.

After a while, his wet clothes gave him chills, and he got up to walk along the sand. He pulled out of his shirt pocket a now moist pack of cigarettes. He tried lighting one, and after several attempts, gave up and tossed it away. As he moved along, he felt the magical charm of a memory. As if his mind were playing tricks on him again, this time with magic. He delighted in recalling Mari Olga's soft, sensuous body. The sea breeze: her breathing. The ebb and flow of the tide: the way she walked. He desired to be on her porch and see her smile at him. It excited him to think about walking with her to the café. He cleared his voice and without caring how off-key he sounded, he sang a few words from a song that reminded him of that cloudy September sky.

> *If they told me to make a wish,*
> *I'd prefer a cloud's whip,*
> *a whirlwind on the ground,*
> *and a great rising anger,*
> *a sweeping sadness,*
> *a downpour of revenge,*
> *and when it clears, hope appearing...*

He paused to look at the sea and repeated in his hoarse voice: *hope appearing after the sunset's shadow.* In the distance, the horizon was shifting continuously in a single direction, deceptively. He smiled, believing he had felt the subtle vibration of the earth beneath his feet, and the joyful breeze kept dancing in love.

♥ ☼ ♥

www.ingramcontent.com/pod-product-compliance
Lightning Source LLC
Chambersburg PA
CBHW032009170626
46807CB00006B/2723